MW01483990

The SILVER™ RECORD

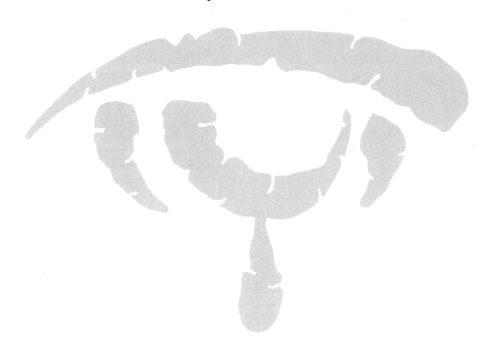

By Bill Bridges, Phil Brucato and Ethan Skemp

Credits

Authors: Bill Bridges, Phil Brucato and Ethan Skemp
Developer: Ethan Skemp
Editor: Aileen E. Miles
Art Director: Aileen E. Miles
Glyph Design and Illustration: Richard Thomas
Layout, Typesetting & Cover Design: Aileen E. Miles

Authors Dedication

Phil Brucato:
This work is respectfully dedicated to Julia "Butterfly" Hill, who has lived in a tree for well over a year as of this writing to protest clear-cutting ancient forests. Many people speak. Few dare to act.

Bill Bridges:
To Jane.

735 Park North Blvd.
Suite 128
Clarkston, GA 30021
USA

© 1999 White Wolf Publishing, Inc. All rights reserved. Reproduction without the written permission of the publisher is expressly forbidden, except for the purposes of reviews, and for blank character sheets, which may be reproduced for personal use only. White Wolf, Vampire the Masquerade, Mage the Ascension and World of Darkness are registered trademarks of White Wolf Publishing, Inc. All rights reserved. Werewolf the Apocalypse, Wraith the Oblivion, Changeling the Dreaming, Hunter the Reckoning, Werewolf the Wild West, and The Silver Record are trademarks of White Wolf Publishing, Inc. All rights reserved. All characters, names, places and text herein are copyrighted by White Wolf Publishing, Inc.

The mention of or reference to any company or product in these pages is not a challenge to the trademark or copyright concerned.

This book uses the supernatural for settings, characters and themes. All mystical and supernatural elements are fiction and intended for entertainment purposes only. Reader discretion is advised.

For a free White Wolf catalog call 1-800-454-WOLF.

Check out White Wolf online at

http://www.white-wolf.com; alt.games.whitewolf and rec.games.frp.storyteller

PRINTED IN THE USA.

The *Silver* Record ™

Contents

Book One: Excerpts from the Record

Book Two: The Language of Glyphs

Unfurling the Scrolls

Glory grows from Inspiration.
Inspiration grows from The Song.
Sow the Song, and Glory will Blossom.
Tend the Song, and Glory will Grow.
— Galliard saying

Well, yes, as a matter of fact, it *is* skin.

Black Spiral hide, to be precise. Tanned with blood, piss and clear water, and purified by a host of secret rites until the Wyrm-taint has been washed away. It's not easy, but I think it's worth the effort. See, the way I look at it, we're reclaiming our lost brothers and sisters for Gaia. It's an honor, really, a respect given to the White Howlers they once were. Maybe, by purifying their skins and writing our greatest legends across them, we're setting their souls free from the Black Spiral and bringing them back to the family.

Yeah, I did say "family" — even the Dancers are still family. We're brothers and sisters, we Changers, despite our tribal differences. We fight with each other like all hell, but the blood in our veins is the same, Mother-blessed and sacred. So be careful how you spill it, brother, and don't do so without a good reason. Dancers and Abominations deserve to die, true, but they should be killed as a mercy, not as an act of malice. Until we reclaim them for our Mother, they're wandering souls, spinning around in an eternal Labyrinth unless some act of mercy sets 'em free.

And no matter what other people tell you, we *are* merciful. It's just that Nature's idea of mercy is a little bloodier than Man's.

By human standards, the idea of skinning someone and writing legends on the hide is pretty savage. I don't think we've ever made a pretense of being anything *but* savage, but there's a deeper level to my madness. As you've probably heard, there's an innate connection between an object and its source. In the case of a skin, there will always be a bond between the leather and the creature from which it came — and between that creature's skin and its soul — even when that soul has left its body. In the case of my Silver Record, that skin connects our lost siblings with the deeds of our past, the spirits of our fellowship, and the Changing Blood which binds us all. So what looks like barbarism is an act of respect, when you take the long view.

The glyphs written across that leather are ancient mnemonics, based on gashes made across bark or stone and inhabited by loyal spirits. To run your hand across them is to literally touch history — to feel the raised lines of the past and invite yourself into the dreams of older days. I've made these marks from ink — ink made the old way, from berries, blood and ashes, not bought down at K-Mart — but I've marked them in my heart the way another Keeper might have carved them in stone. Each glyph represents a slew of memories and impressions. In a way, I've lived through every one of them. Yeah, I may look young, but years are no way to gauge a lorekeeper. If we didn't live the tales we tell, those tales would be as worthless as yesterday's newspaper.

As for myself, well, you can use my human name, Brian, if you want. But these days, I usually go by Wyrm-Takes-Last. It's a mouthful, but it's more in keeping with my duties, and a great man gave it to me. I guess I *do* seem a little young to be carrying around a backpack full of skin-scrolls, but in the last days of the world, you do what you have to do.

That's what we're all about, you know: Doing what you have to do. And that's why we have the Silver Record. In its way, it tells us how.

What is the Record?

You've probably heard of the Silver Record. Most of our Folk have, if only in passing. It's got a reputation that in some ways outstrips the deeds contained within. Some consider it a bible, others a fable, and still others an Academy Award for killing people. But the true Silver Record is none of these things. Rather, it's a combination history book, behavior guide, family album and gospel. It's a road map for our People, and an account of where we've been.

Long ago we, like most tribal folks, kept oral histories. The Galliards of each sept preserved simple chants, rhymes and tales, then recited them at the moots. Depending on the moot, the lorekeeper might retell the deeds of great heroes, tell a story of compassion, or raise an old war-chant to drive his people into a frenzy. Although they preserved old legends, these stories were pretty much custom-made; each lorekeeper had a slightly different spin on what happened. Some Galliards preferred to remember the great deeds a given hero performed — how Gunderthorn Vargarssun strangled three fomori to death with his own intestines, for instance — while another would emphasize the sacrifices he made — the pain he endured while he fought, the tearful farewell he made before expiring — and still another would play up the importance of his deed — how Gunderthorn was all that stood between the Wyrm-things and the sacred Spring of Merraton. Each lorekeeper would phrase things a little differently, customizing them for his audience or tailoring them to the occasion. Even so, the core of the legend — that Gunderthorn died valiantly after killing a pack of Wyrm-spawn with his own guts — was passed on, and endured.

Far later, when people began to write their legends down, many Galliards did the same. It probably seemed like blasphemy to some old-fashioned types, but my guess is, it was a practical decision. After all, we're born to fight and die, and usually do both pretty frequently. If your lorekeeper gets gutted during a fight, 500 years of oral history drains away with his lifeblood. As our people developed the simple but powerful glyphs we all use, each lorekeeper's tales were written down in a simple memory-script. The stories were still open to interpretation, but the core of each one was saved for later tale-tellers' use.

Some say that the original glyphs were strictly fetishes — marks designed to hold spirits — as some of them in the Record still are today. Some even say that the glyphs *were* spirits, that their very shapes and forms were alive and could swim across the surface they were written upon. The Old Lore tells us that to read such a glyph was to receive pure understanding of the image or concept it embodied, with no muddled meaning or multiple interpretations allowed — no slew of post-modern "texts," read any which way the viewer desired. Knowledge was then an objective thing, as real as a tree or stone.

But that was before the Gauntlet. Before that wall of mist and unknowing separated bodies and minds from their spirits. After this sundering, nobody was sure about anything anymore — appearances no longer mattered. People could now lie.

Before the Gauntlet, only Tricksters had the knack of lying — or the Tall Tale, or the Truth Bending, whatever spin you want to put on it. After the spirits went away, anybody could lie — especially humans. With no internal or external spiritual compass to guide them, humans turned to the Weaver for guidance, and created logic and reason to master the confusion of a now empty and meaningless material world.

Instead of a pictogrammic or ideogrammic writing, their increasingly abstract minds — unmoored and unrooted in spirit — devised phonetic alphabets, figures which no longer suggested the images seen in the world around them. Humans really began living in worlds of their own, mental spaces constructed from abstract imaginings rather than the world given to them by their senses. Technology soon followed. Of course, the Glass Walkers revel in this process. They claim whole new spirits are contacted and even created by technology.

I'm not here to bash the whole of human history — I am a homid myself, after all. Born of human parents. Their history is my history. But the way I see it, what happened, happened. There's no going back. The trick is to reconnect today with that old consciousness we lost, that primal synergy of the senses where the spirits play.

Before I ramble again on wild polemics, let's get back to the telling of the tales, the heart of the matter at hand. Each tribe — each pack, for that matter — keeps its own histories. Some groups (especially the ones who prefer nice neat archives, like the Silver Fangs and Furies) keep really detailed, written records. Other groups (especially ones who favor their animal side, like lupus packs and the Red Talons in general) prefer oral records to written ones. Most write down their most important legends, though. Some things are just too valuable to trust to chance. And so the Silver Record was created, bit by bit. As tribes came together, their lorekeepers shared their most inspiring legends. Someone wrote 'em down, and the rest was literally history.

That history is pretty extensive… and heavy, too, I might add. The bunch of scrolls I'm carrying contain just a tiny fragment of the stories I have heard and seen. Some remain in safe-keeping, others are written down in secret hiding-places, and still others have been entrusted to a handful of friends until I can get around to putting the legends into glyphs. Every so often, though, I come out of hiding to share a few of my favorite stories to someone who needs to hear 'em.

Now isn't it just your lucky day?

If you're expecting some sort of history book — "on such-and-such a date, this great Garou did this wonderful thing" — think again. That's human thinking, and if you've made it this far you know how wrongheaded that can be. If you're hoping for literal facts, you won't find them here, either. The Record is a document of experiences, a captured dream of past lives and embellished accounts. Some of 'em, I saw myself during out-of-body journeys in which I fought beside the First Pack or faced down dragons in the Russian snows; others are second- or even third-hand accounts, tales told around a fire long after the echoes of battle had died away. Since I became the Record's keeper, I've been on a quest to uncover as much lore as I could find… one way or another. On that quest, I've heard many tales that would have been lost to me otherwise, and not all of the sources were exacting, reliable, or "literal" in their interpretations. So be it. We're not always able to choose the facts we want. Sometimes in history, as in life, we get what comes our way, and are grateful for that much. Besides, this is oral lore, a collection of tales told 'round the circle. In such tales, poetic embellishments, fables and symbolism can be more truthful than facts and figures.

Besides, you're *Garou*! You live in a world where abstract ideas take literal spirit form. Sometimes the dragon a hero fights is a metaphor for greed, sometimes it's a real dragon, but most of the time for us, it's both — a dragon made out of pure, solid greed. That's why we always have to take the long view.

Despite its name, the Silver Record is not a static collection of written lore. We are a tribal people at heart, and our history is verbal, not written. Like words, it's fluid and moving, a nomad's legacy. There have been many Silver Records, many keepers, many copies of the glyphs and endless interpretations of what they say. Our pictograms are remembrance-devices, really — abstract marks that hold loose meanings and spiritual advisers. The lines themselves mean very basic things — "Wyrm," "danger," whatever. It's up to the reader to interpret the exact meaning and context of a pictograph message. Unlike the sophisticated letters and numbers of modern alphabets, our tribal letters are far more free-form, less "literal" than the constipated words of men.

That said, however, some tales still bear the stamp of their authors. There are idioms that show clearly through the glyphs of old, and the newer generation of tale tellers prefers to put their own stamp on their product, so to speak. It's not very traditional, mind you, but if it gives a Garou some self-respect and renown, I'm all for it.

These scrolls are alive in other ways, too. In the Record, as in some other very important messages, spirits are summoned into the glyphs themselves. When someone runs his hands along the pictograms, the spirit enters him and shows him images of the subject described. To the reader, these seem like vivid dreams or past-life memories. It's kind of freaky, really — if interpreting glyphs is your profession, you acquire a whole set of "shadow memories" of things you've never actually seen. Those of you who have close connections to your past lives know the feeling — that *déjà vu* sensation of living three or four lives at once, none of 'em especially "real" but all of them amazingly clear. Even when the spirits impart their messages and drain away back into the glyphs that hold 'em, the impressions linger. I've lived lifetimes in my less-than-25 years, and I remember more about them than I want to, sometimes. Each time I run my hands across these scrolls, I live them all again. It's not the most comforting feeling in the world, but no amount of words could convey what I see.

Who needs TV?

Traditionally, the Record has been etched in secret chambers — log cabins, lodges, caves, even castles. As I said, there have been many Records, but this one is supposed to be the last. Over the centuries — especially the last few decades — the old Record-homes have been battered down, burned, blown up, or in one really vicious case, turned into a sewage reservoir. The spirits that made those Records live fled into a single cabin deep in the Appalachian woods. A few housing developments later, those woods weren't so deep anymore, and our enemies began closing in on the last Record-home. That's where I came in.

My old mentor, Death-Takes-Last, carved that Silver Record into the walls of his cabin. Eventually, he raised a sept, the Sept of the Hidden Wind, to defend the place. They did a brave job, but it wasn't enough. When agents of the Corrupter closed in on the place, Death-Takes-Last incinerated it to keep its secrets from falling into the hands of Black Spiral Dancers. Although I've been able to recapture some of the tales written on the walls of that cabin, many of them have rejoined their heroes in the ashes of time. After thinking long and hard about what to do, I decided to make these portable scrolls my Record. In these wild times, no single place is safe for very long.

Now I carry the tales with me, literally. In my head, hands and heart, the Record lives. When it dies, we all die with it. But maybe with our deaths, we can buy a new world for our descendants. And perhaps this Record will survive our ashes and bring the word of the old to the world of the new.

Who Am I?

You'll have to bear with me. I'm a Philodox, not a Galliard, and I don't have the traditional loresinger's way with words — or at least I don't think I do. I'm also a lot younger than the traditional Keepers of the Record. I was barely sixteen when the First Change hit me, and I was pretty much grabbed up and set to work the minute the Wolf in me came out.

Why so young? I'm not sure, but I have a few ideas. Maybe it was because I hadn't "found a place" yet. As I quickly discovered, a good lorekeeper has to devote most of his time to uncovering the stories, gathering 'em together, interpreting 'em, setting 'em down in glyphs, and relating 'em to others. It's a full-time job, and not one you can just pick up and run with if you're already set in your ways. Maybe I was chosen to be the Record-Keeper because all the tales would be fresh and new to me — because I hadn't heard 'em a thousand times before, coming out of someone else's mouth. Maybe a fresh perspective is what was needed at the time.

Or maybe my age was a warning. They call me Wyrm-Takes-Last, and I'm supposedly the final keeper. Within my life, it's said, the world as we know it will end. Maybe I'm supposed to be young enough to get a tough job done, energetic enough to impress people with my message, and familiar enough with the modern world to navigate its weirder sides. (Computers, Internet, that sort of stuff. You'd be amazed how few of our kind even know how to turn a PC on… or would *want* to!) When the Apocalypse comes — which I believe it has — anything and everything can be a weapon. As important as tradition is, inflexible attitudes will get us all killed. So perhaps a young Garou was given this task as a warning… or a tool… or even a sign of hope. If I'm destined to live a long life, maybe the End Times aren't as close as they seem. A lifetime, maybe, but not a year or even a decade. Maybe. I hope.

There are other reasons I can think of: Not to get weepy about it or anything, but my home life was pretty screwed up. I was an only child, and didn't have much sense of family. My parents hadn't divorced, but they just as well might have. As it was, they fought like crazy, usually with me in the middle. I learned to be a peacemaker… and a young one, too… the hard way. I guess maybe Gaia figured that if I could make my folks stop fighting, I could get my *true* brothers and sisters to listen up, too. Because trust me, we don't have time to fight. Not anymore.

What Makes Us Family?

Like my mom and dad, our family fights like hell but can never really divorce. In my parents' case, it had a lot to do with they way they were raised — "oath before God," and all that stuff. In our case, the bond runs deeper, all the way down to our spirits and bones. We are bound by the Change, brothers and sisters in Gaia's grace. Although we stand between the three worlds of human, spirit and animal, we are all three in one, in a way that not even the highest animals, most powerful spirits, or most enlightened humans can be. Despite our tribes and traditions, we are all equal in Gaia's sight.

That blood-bond extends much further than we realize. The other Changers — the cats, birds, lizards and all that — were our siblings, too. That's what makes the War of Rage so shameful. It was worse than genocide. It was fratricide, and many of us are still too stupid or dense to admit that. But when you know the Old Songs, when you really understand them, you begin to notice the affinities between us all. And to appreciate the family that binds us and makes us one.

Am I gonna get all moony on you? Uh, uh. I'm no Child of Gaia, and even if I was, the thought of sermonizing like some hippie makes me wanna puke. But there's a truth buried in their bullshit, y'know. That's why, so long ago, they were able to turn back the Impergium and resist the War of Rage. Why they're still alive when a militant tribe like the White Howlers is history... or worse. That truth is pretty simple: We are family. And when we shed a brother's blood, we commit a crime against our Mother. Sometimes, those crimes are necessary. (Look at the brothers and sisters I carry around with me... and yes, as a matter of fact, he *is* heavy, thanks!) Sometimes, the stain of a crime must be washed away by the criminal's blood. Things die so that other things might live — that's simple nature talking. But when we slaughter our siblings, when we kill just because we *can*, we tear holes in our Mother's hide, too. And we weaken her. Make her sick. That sickness becomes a plague, and we all suffer for it. All Changers. All things.

This could be one of the reasons we all stand on the brink of annihilation. Why the Apocalypse is undeniably here. Because our family pulls in opposite directions. It's a curse of the modern world, y'know. Distance from your roots. Don't get me wrong, here. I'm no tree-hugger, and I like cars and the Internet as much as the next guy. But y'see, science is a double-edged razor. It provides us with better ways to feed ourselves, protect ourselves, and move from place to place, but it also breeds isolation and a "me-first" mentality. When people — Garou included — don't feel like they have to struggle to survive, they get soft and selfish. After a while, everyone starts feeling like the lead in their own personal movie. Everyone and everything else in the world becomes supporting cast and background material. At that point, nothing is good unless it enriches you. Unless it makes your life safer, more comfortable, more fun. Don't shake your head, you know I'm right! After a while, nothing in this world matters unless it somehow makes you feel better! Now multiply that by the amount of people in the world today, square it by the economies of nations, and subtract any sort of feeling of community or family. Our family tree is dying — literally! — because we don't feel or feed its roots any longer.

And when it goes, we're going with it.

We need to reaffirm the bonds that make us who we are — know that every single creature under Gaia is who we are, one spirit across space and time. Blood, bone, sap — all one body, all one spirit. We need to be willing to fight for one another, but more importantly, we need to *fight* — because without struggle, without suffering, we'll wither on the vine.

Tribes are important, for they define our kinship. But they also define our differences — and that's a bad thing these days. When we must need to come together, tribal tradition is keeping us apart. I'm sure you can see in this the original squabbles our ancestors had over territory as they migrated across the Turtle's back that is the Earth. And when you think about it, maybe those original fights were important. Maybe things needed some definition then, some boundaries. Life is Balance, and boundaries are important to maintain that Balance. That's what rituals are all about: reaffirming boundaries to maintain the Balance. In this sense, all of life is a great rite.

Tribes are necessary, for they help us to nurture virtues specific to our needs. There's a reason you were born to your tribe and not another's — and that reason is spelled out in all the songs, stories and rituals of your tribe. But knowing that, and cherishing that, it's time we also knew the ways of others and cherished them also.

That's why the Silver Record is for and from all tribes. I don't care if you hate every Shadow Lord you ever met — as the Silver Record shows in a number of stories, without that tribe, the Wyrm would be a hell of a lot stronger. We need them, and they need us (even if they are somewhat reluctant to learn this lesson!). We all come from Mother Gaia, and we're nurtured by Crazy Aunt Luna. We run across the same Mother Earth and howl into the same Father Sky.

Why We Need the Record

The Silver Record does not celebrate bloodsport. It celebrates sacrifice.

A lot of Garou forget that. The Silver Record has been called "The Song of Glory," "The War-Dance Tale," "The Chronicle of All Greatness," and even "Tales of the Bones of Our Enemies." None of those names, as far as I can tell, was given by the Record-Keepers themselves. From the first songs set down by the ancient Galliards, the "silver" in this Record has represented the shine of the moon, the richness of wisdom, the mystery of the twilight, and the wealth that honor brings. It is not, as many people claim, a score-card of dead enemies — we've already got enough of those. To reduce the Record to a pile of skulls is an insult to all who have gone before us. Killing is easy — it's what we were made to do. True wisdom and honor comes from sacrifice. From knowing what is needed, and doing what is needed, especially when you know, going into it, that the right thing to do will cost you. Cost you comfort, cost you blood, cost you everything and everyone you love. Maybe even cost your life, and the lives of those around you. The right thing to do is rarely easy, and it's easily avoided. That's one of the reasons we have the Record: To show those who sacrifice that we do not forget.

Doing the right thing has never been easy, but it gets harder all the time. The more we "civilize" ourselves, the more comfortable we become. When something really big stands knocking at the door (or pissing in the corner, as it were), we find it harder and harder to rouse our lazy asses and go take care of business. Next thing we know, the door is open and our enemy stands in front of us, fangs bared and going for our throat. The more sluggish we become, the harder it is to rouse ourselves to fight. The more comfortable we make ourselves, the easier it is for the enemy to tear out our throats.

We homid-types can learn from what happened to our lupine siblings. Long ago, when people were the minority and wolves pretty much had free run of the place, they got lazy. *Stop* growling, it's the truth! For a while, the Wyrm seemed very far away and the forests seemed to go on forever. Suddenly, as we see in "The Howl for Lost Pack," the people seemed to be everywhere, the woods were disappearing, the food was gone, and the cousins we depend on were being killed off by the hundreds. By the time the wolf-born understood the danger, their full bellies were empty and their pelts hung as trophies on human walls. The Red Talons have made this tragedy a touchstone in their tribal ways, but the lesson of the wolves remains lost: If you grow complacent, the Record tells us, you will die.

Long ago, the wolves were complacent. Now the humans are. But this is no time for complacency. The Apocalypse is upon us, and the next skins on the wall may be our own.

I sometimes think I was chosen for this task because I'm a restless child of the media age (as some people would put it.) If I had been raised in a tribal society, if I had been brought up to revere the Earth and stuff, I might not understand how deeply the modern plague has taken root… and how appealing it can be. If I hadn't spent all my time riding around in cars and watching TV and playing video games and eating McVomit burgers, I might just stand around outside the show and jump up and down and scream my head off wondering why all these terrible things are happening to Gaia. Or squirrel myself away in a cave somewhere carving pictures into walls and moaning about how the Good Old Days are gone, and all. That's not what we need in the Last Days. We need to understand what has led us here, why the road to destruction looks so damned cool. Before you can step off that road, you need a map to see where you've been, and figure out where you're going. I think that's the ultimate purpose of the Silver Record. Not to praise the sunset, but to lead us to the dawn.

Huh. Almost sounded like a real lorekeeper there, for a minute. I never really considered myself the eloquent type, personally. Then again, who am I to question the choices of Gaia or Death-Takes-Last? No one. I'm just the Keeper of the Record, and I've learned that certain questions don't have answers. Sometimes, things just *are*.

Let's run our fingers on the pages, and begin….

The Invocation

Ho! Ho!

Ho! Ho!

    Hokaa say nakwa!

    Hokaa say na-oha!

This is the Record of Wyrm-Takes-Last.

This is the Lore of the People.

This is the Memory of Wolves in the Darkness.

This is the Story of Hope.

Blessed are we

Who live by the Moon's grace.

Blessed are we

Who run with the Sun.

Blessed are we

Who are born by the Earth's grace.

We are the Changers

Of the Warrior Blood.

Seven Times do I Howl,

Seven times do I Sing

Of the Deeds of the People and the Ways of the Moon:

New Moon, for Creation;
Crescent, for Growth;
Half-Moon, for Kindness;
Gibbous, for Sacrifice;
Full Moon, for Valor;
Eclipse, for Shame;
and Bright Moon Again, to Prophecy the New.

Let my Song bear the ages!
Let my voice speak the truth!
I am the Keeper of Quicksilver Twilight.
I am the Bearer of Truth.
Hokhaa ha sola!
Hokhaa say ho!

This is the Lore of the People.
This is the Record of Blood.

New Moon: Creation

I speak of beginnings, of the birth of all things, of the coming of tribes and the giving of Laws. These are the First Songs, the tales of Before. Let all Folk hear them. Let all Folk attend!

We are all kinfolk, members of a family that extends from each stone and particle of air to every living thing. While we Changing Wolves may be the closest blood relations, you must understand that "family" is far greater than we can imagine. Gaia may be our Mother, but all things, living and otherwise, are our kin. Before you can understand the Changing Gift and the Apocalypse, you have to understand the ties that bind us.

Void of Night

This chant comes from an elder of the Wendigo. In my quest, I've heard many creation-tales, but the images that came to me while listening to this chant remain with me, even now.

Ahay-oh!

Ahayy-oh!

I am Darkness.

I am Void.

Ahay-oh!

Ahayy-oh!

I am the mother without children.

I am seedlings yet unborn.

Ahay-oh!

Ahayy-oh!

I am infinite,

Unfathomable,

No meaning, end, or measure.

Ahay-oh!

Ahayy-oh!

I am loneliness, barrenness, and void.

Three stones I grow inside myself,

Three eggs, three glowing coals.

I reach inside, draw them out

And toss them to the empty void where

They burn, so brightly, like fires

In dry leaves or wood.

I watch them for eternities.

Heat becomes warmth, becomes fire, becomes life.

Patient mother, I swim the void and see them grow.

Ahay-oh!
Ahayy-oh!
Darkness is ended.
The Void has fled.
No longer do I drift alone.
Ahay-oh!
No longer am I all alone.
From the fire came the Phoenix,
Witness of my firstborn, my creation.
On flaming wings, she soared across the sky,
Laughed at the fleeing Void,
Laughed to see Creation bloom
Where there was nothing but the night.
Ahay-oh!
Ahayy-oh!
Phoenix laughed to see the end of night.

Songs of the Dawn

Only fragments remain of the other Dawn songs. Here are some of them.

The Three

The flowers opened before the Dawn
Petals spread in silent song
One becomes the green;
One turns the green to tree;
One brings the tree down low,
Decays it, and makes new life from old.
The tree is eternal.
The three are eternal.

First Light

Cold was the world
In eons untold
When time was slow to unfold.
Quicker it became
And faster moved all things
Dancing now in dark delight
Ignorant from lack of sight.
A spark in formless night
Over the hill arose a light
Enflaming aether, igniting air
Color afire in every stare
Vision gifted to every being
Voices upraised, singing
The Sun strode across heaven
Light descended to deepest glen
At break of Dawn,
The Dark withdrawn.

The Trickster Light

As Helios marched,
Creatures awoke from their lairs,
Hatching child from egg,
Opening eye to light and life.
Joyous song and curious croak
Aheard across the fields
As beasts on wobbling feet stood and stumbled
Learning to run.
Over the far hills Helios yet marched,
His light a trail behind him
A mane of fire
Dwindling as on he went.
Air darkened and cooled and night remained
Fear scuttled from holes, chased beings in the cold
But lo another light did dawn
A lesser bright but more subtle silver to the gold of sun
Sneaking from ridge to ridge, stealing Helios' waning light,
Luna came and smote the night.
Seeing her pale, wan light,
Wolves rejoiced, howling away the fright.
Running in packs after dark night,
Chasing down wounded fears,
Tearing hearts with silvered fang,
The wolves raged under shifting moon.

The Naming

This is what the Galliards call a Teaching Tale. A version of this is told among all tribes. This one comes from Death-Takes-Last, my own teacher. I've included it here to stand in for all the variants.

Of the many Powers we know, one is greater than others, for all other Powers follow in its path. It is called Naming, for it is the division from void to form and is the basis of Spirit. This is a Power that belongs only to Gaia, although others have tried to imitate it many times, but all to terrible effect. Only She can use this Power; all other attempts are shadows of Her intent.

The things of the Wyld are Nameless, miasmic in their unshaped chaos and joyful dance, heedless of life, death or any such concerns. The things of the Weaver are likewise unNamed, but the Weaver has given shape to their raw substance. Gaia takes what these two Triat beings have touched, and Names them for Her purpose. In so doing, she makes the things of this world, from stones and bones, plants and trees to wolves and man, and infuses them with Spirit.

The Wyrm has a Power that is nearly as great, for it is Unnaming. It breaks the bonds of Spirit and substance and returns things to the formless Wyld. But the Wyrm is now corrupt, and instead of Unnaming, it attempts to Name on its own, but only creates misshapen beings, for it has not Gaia's wisdom.

Many tales are told of the original Naming, when Gaia gathered all Her creation to her tent to accept the Names she would give every creature. Before this time, all beings were free to take whatever form they desired, and no one could tell anyone apart for sure, for many masks they wore.

It is said that the tricksters heeded not the proper decorum, and stood in line many times, receiving many Names from Gaia, and thus allowing them to imitate more powers and shapes than others. Of course, Gaia recognized them right off, but played as if she didn't know who they were, coming around like children begging more candy. She knew their curiosity would get them into trouble, and that they would need more than one Name each to escape the wrath of those they tricked.

The Changing Breeds each got two Names. One is the Name of Man, and the other that of the beast they favor. Some envied the Changers their double status, but others drew away from them, wisely aware that to be doubly-Named is to be doubly beset with trouble.

If this is so, you say, then how is it with those men who are mighty in Power unlike the rest of their kind? What of them? The mages know their own Names, or perhaps it is that their Names know them. This is what gives them their Power.

The Leeches have been Unnamed, losing a part — but not all — of their original Name. And the fey? They are figments given form, fictions born from dream. They were not Named in Gaia's tent, but in Her dreams. As such, they are not always what She intended, but continue to delight Her as a wondrous dream does for us.

23

The Old Days

A song about life after the Dawn. It's not easy to date all these tales, especially those as old as this, but I think this one actually comes from the waning of those elder days, since the singer is trying to get others to understand what they should already know but have forgotten.

To see the face of immortality, you must leave the human world behind.
This fire, these woods, the wind in the branches overhead,
This is the true world, the Mother's realm,
The seat of the immortal, the heart of our world.
The Weaver spins a gilded web, and strong, but it is false,
Ephemeral, when placed against the branches or the flames.
Steel and glass give brave assurances, but only viewed against our
        fragile flesh.
Inside that flesh, inside ourselves, is immortality,
The shard of our past lives, the seed of our tomorrows,
And to that flesh, the Weaver's gifts are not more lasting
Than the curling smoke from the fire we now share.
To touch the face of our immortal Mother,
You must reach beyond the comforts you have known.
Speak your prayers into the shallow waters,
Send your essence through the glass.
For the Immortal Ones have shown us the path to their domain,
To the heart of immortality, we glide like shadows.
Like errant cubs, we return to our home.
Listen now, to the rustle up above;
Breathe the heavy scent of pine and forestfall;
Close your eyes, forsake the things you "know,"
As I speak of bygone times, and of the world we once were born to.
    Hey yaaa! Hiiii-oh!
    Hey yaaa! Hey yaaa, hiiii-oh!

When the skies were huge and dark at night,
Unlit by cities' restless blaze,
Brightened only by the glowflies' dance,
The stars, and the crackling of our fires,
And the air was thick with green tree-breath
The fleeting tear of burning wood,
We hunted those days like the wolves we are,
And sung by night like the men we may be.
Those days were not easy, oh my brothers, oh my sisters!
Let no one delude you that they were so.
Cold and toil ever were our lot, and
We measured the seasons in the deaths of friends.
Never was this world a paradise; it is
Built on bones and briars.
Death has always been the seed of life,
And pain lends sharpness to our senses.
But once, these things were pure; death
Followed in his season like an alpha to his queen or
Lightning to an oak that would rise again some day as
Saplings fed by dying wood.
For thus is Nature's way.
If paradise there be where all is happiness and bliss,
It resides there in some Otherworld where
Lessons learned in this
Land have blossomed into greater sense.
Life, my siblings, is a mountain we must climb.
Those who flounder at its slopes may be mourned or pitied
But they cannot bring the mountain down,
And must not be allowed to.
Like worms in a rotting carcass or
Termites in the wood, some seek to corrupt
What they cannot enjoy; from these, we take our supper.
For thus is Nature's way.

The Rending of the World

There are a lot of stories telling us how the world got to be in the screwed up shape it's in. This is one of them, and it traces our predicament way back to ancient times, to that moment when the Wyrm went mad. The story doesn't tell why he went mad, but we all know different versions of its fall from balance. In fact, there's no official version of it anywhere in the Record. I think this is because nobody really knows for sure, and nobody wants to get close enough to the mad dragon to find out.

Once, the world was a single land, a plain that stretched from the ends of the sun to the edge of the moon, and covered all places in between. Deep pools and rivers cut through this land, keeping it pure and green, and bottomless oceans surrounded this land on all sides.

In his rage, the Wyrm cracked the shell of the world into many pieces; some floated off into the sea and sank. Others became islands, while the larger pieces became the continents. The skies were filled with thunder as the Dragon split the world apart, and great mountains fell at his command. At the shores, the seas overflowed their banks and washed across the beaches, drowning all that lived upon them. Jagged shards of the world smashed upward through the crust, shattering forests and turning them to sand. The very moon and stars shifted in their orbits, and the Velvet Shadow was torn. With a scream like ten thousand souls in pain, the Wyrm shrieked and tore his claws through the world. In their wake, the lands of flesh and spirit were divided forever.

What was once one became many. What was once whole became broken. Weep as she might, Mother Gaia could not undo this terrible thing. Luna comforted her, but could not change the deed.

So wrought with despair was Gaia that she took to her bed in sorrow, and would not walk among the fields and trees or oceanbeds that she once carefully shaped. She was afraid to see the ruin made of her work. Without her presence and caretaking, the world grew even worse.

In the wake of the Wyrm's rampage, rifts which may have been sealed by Gaia's healing hand lay rotting open to the air. Bleeding stones and cracked rivers could not mend their wounds, and cried for the Mother to heal them. This crying only made Gaia weep the more, and sapped her strength such that she could no longer rise.

Luna saw this and shook her head, her pity long since dried up. She set to work in Gaia's place, going where she could and spreading her luminous radiance to all quarters. But while she could go where Helios refused, her light was dimmer than his, and could not reveal all the damage the Wyrm had wrought. She needed helpers in her task.

She went first to the Bear Changers, but they were asleep, healing the grievous wounds they had suffered defending the land from the Wyrm. She then went to the Crow Changers, but they flew close to Helios and would not leave him. She then went to the Wolf Changers, who roamed the blasted land in packs. Only they greeted her with respect, glad they were to see her light. She begged of them her favor, and they readily accepted.

She sent them far and wide into the sundered realms to be her eyes and ears, witnesses to the destruction and harbingers of healing. Even though the realms of spirit were now sundered from matter, she taught them the way to attain passage to these places, and bid her spirits erect the Moon Paths across landless regions.

As they roamed ever farther, the wolves howled report to the moon and their fellow packs. Hearing these voices of surety and valor, spirits clamored to the Wolf Changers and saw in them protectors and menders of the world. Alliances they pledged and friendships they forged with the wolves which have not been forgotten to this day.

And as the howls were heard more frequently, as more and more realms were rejoined, Gaia sat up in wonder at the sounds. She threw off her blanket of sorrow and moved into the world, seeking the source of the mighty howls.

Her coming forth was a new spring, and life bloomed again in the wake of her passing. Clouds dispersed, and Helios shone through to the earth, drying its dewy tears. Gaia came upon a pack of Wolf Changers and smiled to see them, and bent down to them to speak in the alpha's ear: "You shall be my protectors hence forth, and defend my creation from ruin. Whenever I rest, you shall roam untiring, heralds of my will."

And so it was that the Wolf Changers became first in Gaia and Luna's favor from among all other Changing Breeds.

And the Wyrm? Its rampage wore at its strength, and it slithered into a deep trench its jaw had dug into the earth, and curled up and slept. But its dreams unfurled nightmares from the mists of unbeing to the clay of matter, creating monsters which rampaged in its stead upon the earth. These did the Garou hunt and slay, but they were many.

And as the dragon slept, the Weaver sent her Spider Incarna to sneak upon him and devise a cage to hold him, so that he might not escape his proper work of balance again. But the snake awoke before the Weaving was complete, and thrashed about, flinging webs everywhere, strands which wrapped about the Spider and Wyrm alike, catching both in the trap. Then did the Wyrm work its way through the sticky pattern and swallow the Spider like a thrashing mouse, and in so doing, swallowed a piece of the Weaver also.

Ever since, the Weaver has been mad, sharing the Wyrm's rage and disbalance. But the Wyrm has shared alike in the Weaver's power, and tries to make patterns of its own, but the warp and woof are ragged and ill-sewn, creating only corrupt things.

27

The Others

I've assembled a variety of legends here. Except for the one about the vampires, which is the oldest, the others are a patchwork I put together myself. No one song speaks of magi, faeries, vampires and ghosts together. So, in the interest of addressing what many of our kind regard as pressing matters, I worked a jumble of old songs together and strove to give them some semblance of similarity. If the result seems lopsided, sue me. I'm no poet, I'm a diplomat.

Leeches

Woe to you my cub who has seen the blood-drinkers stride proudly about the night, protected in their electric demesnes by blood-bound witness and dark Gifts. I will tell you who they really are, so that they cannot fool you again. Never give them succor or even pity; instead, give them over to the Sun, so that he might enact his ancient vendetta against them.

It was so long ago that no ancestor who witnessed the event can be called, and so we rely on the witness of spirits and lore protected over time. Humans were abundant and only beginning to show signs of their Weaver allegiance. The Impergium was yet to come. Yet, the Weaver was impatient, waiting for men to come to her ways, for of all Gaia's children, they were the most suited to her. But every time she tried to sway them, the Garou would arrive to draw their Kin back into proper accord, teaching through fang and claw.

So, the Weaver decided to make her own being, one who would serve her fully, without any Garou kin to claim it. Unable to fire the spark of life on her own, she stole a human and wove webs about him, making him wholly her own. In doing so, however, she snuffed out his spark, so that his spirit fled. But it could not escape the thickly-woven cocoon of webs about it, and was thus trapped to inhabit its own husk. The body soon began to rot, and the being begged the Weaver with syrupy tongue to save it from the stench and dissolution. She could not resist his pleas and wove into his being immortality.

He grew greedy for more power, and used guile to trick it from her. He stole from her with pleas and whines many secrets to the Patterns in the world, so that he could unravel some webs or stitch still others.

But the Wyrm saw this, and knew it was wrong. Seeking balance, it swallowed the Undead Man, to return it to the cycle of being. He could not digest him, however, for the thing was undying. Sitting in the dark womb of the Wyrm's gut, the Undead Man grew hungry, but the only thing to eat was the blood flowing in vessels around it. So it bit into the swiftly moving fluid and sucked strongly of its nourishment.

The Wyrm writhed in pain and fear, and spat out the blood-sucking meal. The Undead Man, covered in the Wyrm's blood, was a horror to see. All beings who saw it averted their eyes and groaned in terror. Gaia herself could not look at the thing, so corrupt was its demeanor.

Helios looked down upon the blasphemous Bloody Man and smote him, igniting his flesh in painful flame. The Bloody Man dug screaming into earth, climbing down into a tunnel far from the sun's gaze. Only this protected him from Helios's anger, and the dirt about him smothered the flame.

Gaia cursed the Bloody Man then, and said: "Although you came once from my loins and have a spark of the Wyld in you, it has been smothered by the Weaver's webs. Because of this, you cannot change or die, except by the Power of spirits or other magical beings. What is worse, you will think this tragedy a blessing, and hunger to stay unchanged for all time. But think not that you will remain ever awake, for nothing that is can evade sleep and dream. But your sleeps will be mighty, and last ages, so that when you waken, all will have changed but you, and your dreams will be only nightmares.

"Because the Wyld is weak in you, no children will you bear. Because you have fed from the blood of the Great Devourer, you must corrupt others to make them your own. Only through death can you mold life. All my children will bear only fear for you."

And then Helios's voice thundered down from the heavens: "Show not your face again to me, or I will smite it. And should you corrupt others to your purposes, them too shall I smite."

The Wyrm was dizzy and weak from blood loss ever afterwards, and grew worse and worse when its internal wound did not heal. Everyone knows that story and what came next. But the Bloody Man was forgotten, for he had fallen into a deep sleep in the earth. Only in later ages did he arise again to corrupt others, creating generations of awful beings like him.

He is still alive today. No one has seen him, but no one has seen his husk or spirit either.

The Magi

In the days of feast-slaying, when the wolves
Tore out the hearts of men,
Some humans, by the fire kissed,
Learned great arts and brought the stars to earth.
Some made great things for their fellow folk —
Others crawled into darkness and made love unto the worms.
In the old days, it has been said, four siblings spoke
In great voices: one mad, another stone,
The third one midnight and the fourth one sane.
Two walked in a sacred way;
One danced amid the flames, and the last ate her own heart.
The sacred ones birthed vision-children, whose
Cauled heads bespoke a greater sight:
Some spoke to spirits as we did;
Some brought the thunder down alone;
Some built great lodges of brick and briar;
Some walked the paths of ghosts.
In the fires, the mad one cried;
In the darkness, the heartless one conspired.
All one blood, they stood alone,
And plucked the Weaver's threads for warmth.
Sometimes we made war upon them,
Other times, we shared our hunts.
The sacred ones made hearths for our human hearts,
And sometimes learned the gifts of skin-change.

With their help, the humans spread.
Soon this was the cause of war.
For the sacred ones rose up against the
Necessity of our hunts.
We shed one another's blood
Until our elders counseled truce.
For the sacred ones are the voice of Man,
Though they court the Weaver's home.
When the Impergium fell, we buried our spite
Until the nights
That the sacred ones came thirsty to our glens....

The Dreaming Ones

I had a dream one night, I think,
And awoke to see it standing by,
All covered o'er with silver flame;
I cringed to see it there.
When I looked again, it was gone,
Dancing off across the hills and laughing
Like a stream.

Each night, whole realms are born, to vanish at the pricklings of day.
Each day, the trees whisper with new shapes and odd designs.
And of the realms both light and dark, new People take their
      form and frame.
Some are of day-terrors born; when frightened musings
Seek comfort in the night; they advance the darkness' call
And try to bind the sun away.
Others, hatched by toils of the day,
Take kinder shapes and bring the sun with them;

As their cousins banish the bad dreams of dayshine,
So these banish vagaries of night.
Once was there war between both night and day,
And even Gaia's chosen trembled.
Old Luna looked upon these dreams with fear and humor mixed;
So inventive were her children, yet neither night nor day could win.
So she divided each dream with her hands,
Making each a mirror of the other:
"So will it be," she said, "so is my gift."
And thus the war was stilled; it continues on
Each day and night, but at a kinder pace; at times
The armies switch their hearts and come to an accord.
For such is Nature's way.

The Restless Ghosts

Those lost souls who found no garden,
No bite of blood-Wyrm to bind their souls,
Built palaces of spirit-stuff, ephemera
To shelter from the winter cold,
For a tempest roars beneath the earth, a suck-hole
Of human terrors and greed;
We soar above its whirlpool when we die, but
Humans are made of weaker things, and
Fall into this tempest, and are torn by winds of fear.
As the Unmaker grows, this tempest swells
And drives the ghosts back to the living lands.
A corruption of Nature's ways.
To these, our elders spoke amid the trappings of the dead;
They ventured to the land beyond the sun.
With corpse-dust and rattle-bones, they raised
An eerie howl and sought to lay the Restless Ones
At peace.
But the Restless would have none of this;
They built a wall against our cries.
No longer could our people cross the paths of death,
(although the Striders found a way).
Within their walls of stone, the Restless built
A city, with the Weaver's aid.
Its battlements were forged of suffering souls;
Its gates, of whispering shades.
And they barred its passage against our kind,
Life and death remained apart,
And this too is Nature's way.

Crescent Moon: Growth

These tales are about the Garou's early days, when culture was not yet set into hard tradition as it is for us today. They're reveal something about events which help define who we are still, whether it be a coming-of-age chant or a bunch of Ragabash learning new tricks.

Lot'a-ha-Khenn (Shaking Paws) Becomes a Man

This is one of the oldest songs I have learned, an ancient Croatan celebration. As far as I can gather, Lot'a-ha-Khenn was a small gray wolf who had a hard time following his pack into battle. His name, Shaking Paws, brands him a coward. As we can see, he overcame whatever issues he had, and was the only one to emerge from the "Fallen Star Land." (Obviously a Hive of some kind.) Although the details about "Khil-to" and his twelve Dancers are lost to me, we can assume he was a real badass. Lot'a-ha-Khenn obviously got mauled in the fight and probably earned a few major battle scars. We don't know anything about Shaking Paws' packmates (their Mourning Howl has been lost to me), but in the obvious joy of the lore-keeper, we can see how Shaking Paws had raised himself from a despised coward to an honored septmate by a single, if costly, act of courage.

All gather! All gather!
All dance! All Dance!
Dance to the honor of Lot'a-ha-Khenn,
Who has killed the Things-Below-Ground!
With his full moon talons and his silent feet,
He has gone to the Fallen Star Land
And returned with clutches of black bones and furs.
See his skin! Once gray
It has been stained red as embers!
See his eyes! Once afraid,
They have looked into fires!
See his limbs! No longer
Do they shake with fear!
His eyes are sad, but he is a man!
His packmates are gone,
His packmates are fallen,
His skin has been scarred with the brand of Khil-to!
But he has returned,
Returned to us!
And in his hand, he has brought the bones of Khil-to
And in his teeth, the skins of twelve Dancers!
No longer is he Shaking Paws!
From this day, he is Slays-With-Heart!
So dance to the honor of Lot'a-ha-Khenn!
Sing to the moon for the price he has paid!
Catch his tears in your hands,
Taste the salt that they bear,
For Lot'a-ha-Khenn has returned
And now he is a man!

The Golden Tiger and His Mistress

You'll never catch me lauding the War of Rage, but if you know something about the deeds that inspired it, it's easier to understand why it happened. This fragment, part of a Silent Strider epic called "The Sixty-Five Virtues," recalls the early War and the evil that helped begin it. Told by a war-judge of the Eaters of the Dead, this tale marks a pact between Silent Striders and Red Talons somewhere in the vicinity of India. In time, this alliance would spread and become one of the most powerful forces in the War of Rage. And all because of a Bastet who had to play king-for-a-day!

I put this story here rather than in the collection of shameful tales because the War marks the first time (and last time) large numbers of Garou collaborated on any single thing. Anyone wondering why we're losing to the Wyrm should take that little fact and ponder it a bit!

Thee Savatr, whose three golden heads hath seared the dawn, art strong and three times Mighty. Excellent is thy gaze, and many are the fruits of thy four splendid Kinfolk, for here in the barren sun are we left alone!

Dear friend, most luminous, turn to us as the Golden Tiger Jamadagni and his Mistress, the dark woman Sa'ar, bring down their claws upon us! For the stones in the hands of the six-score men of the tribe of Sa'ar wound us hatefully! And the blades of the Tiger rend our flesh into carrion-straw, that the birds do carry it away and make nests of our bones!

Oh, Savatr, Resplendent Friend whose howl doth unfurl the crows from their branches, grant us audience and respite! Thine pack doth shine like bolts in the Sky; thine anger affronts the coiled serpents in their secret homes. For thine aid we call an end to the bitter flood that hath parted our domains! For thine goodwill we do offer nine hundred nights of hospitality and the rights to First-In-Speech. Pride is but a flood in a rainy season, and it sweepeth all away who would make shelter on its shores.

And Savatr, he rises aloft like a thundercloud and shakes the mountain with his ten thousand cries.

And his host doth likewise join the tide, and forsake the blood of brothers for the blood of tigers and of men.

And we like strong winds strike. As the day slides into darkness, the eyes of man fall dead and their ears ring with terror's confusions. For man was not born to night as wolves and tigers were, and their fire is a lure to the teeth of after-day. Like a storm we blast the homes of man into timbers and scatter their seeds into fallow fields. Sweet harvest, that ever thus is ours!

To the ground we send the tigers, though they wet the soil with our spill and chew our throats to froth. For Savatr has come; and with him his three heads Varnua, Keth-saya and Prsni. Their breath is like hymns to thunder, and their teeth shine like polished rain. Sharp-pointed and vigorous, we harry the tribe of Jamadagni, and slay their allies also.

For the Golden Tiger hath friends among the night-bloom. In solitude, these shadows come among us, butchering like sleeping birds the Kin of our two packs. And so to such falls Prsni, whose blood takes root and gives forth fruit which, in the way of plants, points to its planter like an accusing hand. And so falls Daksina, most beloved of Savatr, whose bones take root and become a twilly-tree. Beneath that tree, our Friend sits each night, weeping salty lamentations and promising kind-for-kind. So we feel the pain of shadows, and thus hunt them we to their deaths.

The shadow-cats fall like rotten fruit from trees already blooded. Their moonrakes are like serpent's teeth, and shimmer in the half-world light. Speaking in sweet rhymes, they come to our Kin in mockery, saying Where art thine elders, that we could so easily come upon thee? And Where art thine protectors, that we would know thy secrets even if you speak not them? Like black flames come they into our packs, slaying those whom they might reach and corrupting those whom they might beguile.

And so the Golden Tiger's war becometh bloody sunset. Confounding the shadow-cats with Middle-Walking, Savatr and Keth-saya, and Inka-Ten of our own Tribe, go among them as they sit planning their deceptions, and bring them all to blood and ruin.

Truly do the children water their Mother's bosom!

Oh Resplendent Friend, we have brought the Golden Tiger down! Oh Resplendent Friend, we have slain his helpmates and his children! Oh Resplendent Friend, we have returned the lands of Sa'ar to forest and turned pale soil dark with her kinsmen's blood! Rise like a falcon, Bright Savatr, whose coat recalls the sunrise! Rise that we might feed the crows with the flesh of all our rivals!

Deathless friends, let the bright skulls of our slain be the find-fires of our future nights. Let the brains of foemen be our repast, that we might know the lies that led them. Let their dust be carried off by flies and rolled by the scarabs in their sightless tasks.

Our pact is sealed. Go thou in peace! Let the goodwill of our promises be the seed of new tomorrows.

Evil comes to the Mocking Trees

Tricksters rarely work well together. When a group of habitual contraries try to form a pack, they usually dissolve into chaos. One legendary exception, the Mocking Tree Sept, proved that Ragabash could work together well… so long as someone provided enough joke-fodder to satisfy them all.

"You are too full of humor," said the elder to Fee-ne-nee. "You are too brash," said another elder to Jack Stinkbean, "and your breath is horrible!" "You are a coward," said one silly wise man to Always-Going-South, "and cannot belong to our pack. Begone!" These three tricksters all met in the forest where Veeho the Silent made his home. And there, they thought to make sport of one another.

"I can make my eyeballs fly out of their sockets and roll around that tree," said Always-Going-South. So saying, he sent his eyes out of his head and up into a tree.

Fee-ne-ne laughed at him and said "That's nothing. I can make my arms and legs go in all directions, crawl up the tree, take your eyeballs and run away with them!" At that, her arms and legs all fell off and scurried up the tree. One fist grabbed Always-Going-South's left eye. The other fist grabbed his right eye. The two legs came together and the two arms jumped up to meet them. With the eyes well in hand, they ran out of the tree and disappeared into the forest. Fee-ne-ne laughed, her torso bouncing up and down on the grass. Always-Going-South was angry. He shouted and shrieked and tried to kick Fee-ne-ne's torso, but with his eyes in her fists he was blind, and could not see her.

Jack Stinkbean burped (as he often did), and his breath singed the trees black as smoke. The leaves all turned into ashes and fell in piles to the ground. There, not far away, stood Fee-ne-ne's arms and legs, holding the eyeballs.

Veeho the Silent said nothing. His mouth never moved. But the trees around them laughed. At the sound, the birds flew away, taking the arms and legs and eyeballs up into the sky. As they flew, the birds shat out great piles of droppings, which fell on the head of Jack Stinkbean.

"Hey!" shouted Always-Going-South. "Bring back my eyes!"

"Hey!" shouted Fee-ne-ne. "Give me back my limbs!"

"Hey!" shouted Jack Stinkbean. "Your birds shat on me!"

And Veeho the Silent stood in the shadows and nodded, for he had shown them who the leader would be. And so they became a pack, and their home became known as the Mocking Trees Forest, because anyone who entered there would be plagued by jests.

Now it came to be that a great shadow fell across the land. A panther-queen, the bloodthirsty Strange Owl Crying, brought the cat-folk together in a most unusual way. For many days, they chased all other beasts from the forests, hunting those they could follow and slowly eating them alive. These cat-folk knew the forests and mountains well, and they were very clever. Six wolf-packs — including the three packs that had cast out their Ragabash — went to fight against Strange Owl's pride, and all of them died badly. Strange Owl Crying filled her den-cave with skulls, and decorated the trees with pelts and dying foes.

When all the animals had been chased away or killed, Strange Owl Crying led her Pumonca pride to the edge of the Mocking Tree Forest. "I will not go in there," said one werecat, "for I have seen a shadow-man ripped limb-from-limb in that place!"

"And I will not go in there," said a second werecat, "for I was once chased 'round and 'round through those trees. Five days was I laughed at and led further into the woods, but never did I see the source of laughter."

"And I will not go in there," said another werecat, "for my mate was driven mad by the insects that plague that place. They bit her until her fur was matted with blood. When she left the woods, the bites itched her so badly that she scratched all her fur off and bled all day and night. At last, she threw herself off a cliff in frustration. If you go in there, my queen, you will go alone!"

"Cowards!" proclaimed Strange Owl Crying in her high and eerie voice. "I will hunt down the source of the Mocking Trees, and we will eat them from their fingers and toes to their hearts, chewing slowly!" And so she went into the woods while the other werecats watched and waited.

Soon the trees echoed with Veeho's laughter. As the werecats listened, they heard Fee-ne-ne's arms and legs scurrying among the branches. The eyes of Always-Going-South followed Strange Owl as she padded through the forest, and the pack leader's voice taunted her away from where the eyes were hidden. Every so often, the birds would fly off, dropping their shit all over the proud cat's fur. In this way, the Ragabash led Strange Owl Crying deep into their woods.

When she reached the center of the forest, the panther-queen saw Jack Stinkbean sitting alone near a large pool of water. Without a word, the cat-queen sprang at her prey, but Jack Stinkbean knew what was coming. As Strange Owl jumped, Fee-ne-ne's arms tripped the cat. As Strange Owl fell, the Ragabash's legs kicked the panther in the behind. When she snarled and spat at the limbs, they scattered. At that moment, Jack Stinkbean belched.

As the elder had said, Jack Stinkbean's breath was very bad. To make things worse, he had been eating stink grass and drinking fire-water as the cat raged through the forest. Now his breath turned the woods to ashes and toppled the trees around the panther-queen. Her fur caught fire as Jack Stinkbean jumped into the pool. Fee-ne-ne's arms and legs jumped in, too. As Strange Owl Crying burned, Veeho laughed from the trees. Hearing this, the other cats slunk away into the night and never came back.

From that day on, the forest of the Ragabash has been called Cat-Burning-Brightly. Although that happened very long ago, no one has ever tried to conquer those woods again.

Half-Moon: Kindness

Believe me, it's not easy finding tales about kindness among our kind. Oh, they exist all right, but nobody wants to tell them. They've all got tales of blood and guts they want to tell first, and seem disappointed when you want to hear about a simple healing or compassionate sacrifice.

But these are just as much a part of Gaia's work — moreso, in fact — than tales of testosterone and rage. You can really learn something from these, and their heroes make you rethink how we view heroes.

Mud Wolf's Luminous Speech

OM

The universal sound, the basic howl of the universe, is contained in that syllable. Listen to it. Speak it. And feel it vibrate in your heart.

Remember that everything is connected to all other things, such that there are no identities or beings except Gaia. All minds are delusions in a web of desire, anger and shame, formed of warped weavings. All minds exist in truth in the Dharma Gaia and the True Gaia Realm. To think otherwise is to think with the Small Mind, not the Great Heart.

Ah, but it is so hard for the mind to know this, for the heart to grasp it. But it has been done! There is one I know of who attained such a truth, who became one with Gaia yet returned to this world of meat and sorrow to show us our true faces. I will tell you of him. I will speak of Mud Wolf and his Radiant Vajra Voice.

He was of the Changing Breed, a wolf and a man both, of the tribe of Stargazers, those who are most wise to the truth hidden behind veils and enigmas. For many years upon years did he, like others, wage war against physical and spiritual foes, always severing one enemy's head only to see it return with another face. He wondered to himself, 'How can this be? Our enemies are numberless, or else are but One, which hides behind many masks.' He withdrew from quests and battles to contemplate this, taking pilgrimage into the Spirit Worlds to meditate on Moon Paths and at crossroads.

One day as he was contemplating the nature of the Wolf Changer's problem, his mind escaped his body, for so light had it become and so detached from his senses, that it lost its material binding. When this happened, a Bane snuck upon the body and slipped under its fur, claiming the body for its own. The Stargazer was shocked and scared, but then realized how little such a thing mattered. No harm came to his spirit from it. His body was just a metamorphic thing, a figure of clay made to bend in many poses, but not the essential heart of his being. He laughed then to see the pitiful Bane trying to walk in his body, as it stumbled about and attempted to shift forms.

And his laughter peeled away all the strings which bound him. It tore through the webs that covered his eyes, the silk curtain which concealed from him the True Gaia Realm. From this most holy and enlightened perspective, he realized many things which we cannot even conceive of in our ignorant states. But in that timeless time, he grew and achieved the supreme Truth of all Oneness, and realization of the Weaver's deception, and that of her harried victim, the Wyrm.

He chose not to remain in that bliss, for his heart was still one with the Garou. He could not abandon them to delusion, so he returned from that realm, and only moments had passed in the Spirit World, where the Bane still struggled to master his body.

The Stargazer then spoke a word which he had heard in the True Gaia Realms, a tone that thrummed with creation and which was resonant with that Realm from which he had just come, the paradise that hides behind all semblance. And hearing it, the Bane also realized the Truth, and perceived that his struggles were in vain, for nothing it did could possibly corrupt the Incorruptible, the Heart of Gaia that beats beyond all forms.

The Bane grew still, and left the Stargazer's body, and bowed to the being that had freed him. His chains to corruption were severed, but so too was his incarnation in this realm. He faded away, to be reborn again in a new form, one uncorrupted by Wyrm. Another chance it had to attain wisdom on its own.

From there, the Stargazer climbed back into his body, which to his now-luminous eyes was but a thing of clay. He thus took on again the weight of the world's substance and form, its layers of mud, so that he could spread wisdom in that world.

He traveled far in search of those who most needed his teachings, and with his luminous speech, his Radiant Vajra Voice, freed many beings from the Wyrm and Weaver-woven bonds. But every time he did so, the corruption and weight of delusion which they shed was attached to him, but only to his body, never his spirit. It became such that his form was ugly and wrinkled, stinking as if a thousand yeasts grew in his skin. He was truly now the Mud Wolf.

People feared him wherever he went, and would not wait to hear his words or witness his mudras. They fled or attacked, but could not hurt him, only slicing off chunks of his mud body.

This reputation was a good thing, though, for word would reach the vilest Wyrm creatures of a new monster loose upon the earth, a being of stinking refuse and terrible visage who carried the patchwork armor of Wyrm. They sought this being out that they might pledge to him and, under his banner, do delicious evil to Gaia's beings.

And so they came to him, and he did not need to seek them out. And when they bowed and fearfully asked him to patron them, he smiled and spoke words of assent, but words which vibrated at a primal level, and which shattered the souls of these hateful servants and shook them loose from their forms, freeing them to return to the cycle of life and death, now cleansed of all their past corruptions. Their karmic ties did adhere to Mud Wolf, and the uglier he grew, but he was ever master of the husk he bore.

Finally, following visions from Gaia, three wise Stargazers came to him, for they had realized his identity and the good work which he did. They bowed and begged him to speak his words to them, so that they too might see the True Gaia Realm, if even for an instant, before their spirits departed.

He smiled, but said nothing. His eyes closed in contemplation, and the three wise wolves waited for another sign from him, an answer to their pleas. For many days they waited, and the Mud Wolf did not move. Not a bat of his eyelash did they witness, or the slightest pulse of breath in his chest.

Finally, one of them reached forth his walking staff and touched the Mud Wolf on his shoulder. The great Stargazer's misshapen body crumbled at the prod, falling like old, dried clay and clumps of earth. The Stargazer had departed, knowing his work was done. Only his empty form remained, and even that could not last, for there was nothing to hold it together, so completely had Mud Wolf departed the realm of delusion and form. Not a trace of corruption was found in the body, cleansed by its closeness to the truth.

The three Stargazers laughed and wandered off, but they would always tell the tale to all they saw of the Mud Wolf and his supreme compassion, to take on the ills of the world and free creatures from the bonds of delusion, even at the expense of his own comfort.

Some say that Mud Wolf returns now and then, wearing again a body of dirt and clay. If you see him, don't run. Wait and follow, and hope that he speaks, for what he has to say, you greatly want to hear.

The Dawn Flower

There was once a Child of Gaia named Ophelia Beloved-of-Moon who was more beautiful than any other creature on earth, or so those who saw her swear. Her face was surely a mirror of Gaia's own, for from no other source could such beauty arise. Her face and shapely form ignited lust in some, even other Garou, such that they begged her to break the taboos and lie with them. To all she refused, leaving deep scars as warnings in those who were not swayed by her words alone.

Yet she did take husband, a quiet and unremarkable human Kinfolk. His only true love, besides her, was a garden which grew in his large yard. His ancestors had left it to him, and pressed upon him the importance of keeping it alive. And they handed down through his line a priceless seed to be planted only in the direst time. After he died, early even for human years, she tended his garden, and placed her love for him there, for they had had no children, and carried the precious seed always on a string around her neck. Wise in the ways of plant spirits she became, such that she knew all their names, and they came to know her. No other earthly garden, except one yet undiscovered perhaps, grew as green and grand as hers, and sometimes Garou would come visit it, and walk there for solace.

Because there were few among the Garou who were wiser about plants than she, Ophelia was also called the Gardener of the Moon Glade, for such was the name of her husband's garden. And she tended it for many years, growing old as all things of Gaia do. Her fierce beauty went out of her, but was replaced instead by an even greater beauty, but one only the old could recognize, for it was the beauty of wisdom which shone from depths within her spirit. The young packs, unaware of her former glamour, mocked her, for a Garou that pruned vines and flowers instead of fighting the Wyrm was to them a coward. But the elders knew better, and would come to the garden at times to rest and contemplate great things.

Nothing so pure as the Moon Glade can be left unchallenged by the Wyrm, and so it was that fomori came one day to ruin the life within those lawns. They entered her garden in the guise of young humans, bedecked in tattoos and torn shirts, so that if witnesses saw their violence, they would blame it on rebellious youth and only legislate harder against the folly of the young, further widening the gap between generations.

Beset by them in her sanctuary, Ophelia fought hard but could not alone prevail. She howled for help from any nearby kin, for her garden was close to the bawn of a caern.

Devon Dark Brows heard her cry and gathered his pack. His warriors were mighty and merciless, and came suddenly upon the fomori, tearing into their flesh with a rage unbound. They soon destroyed all the marauders in the garden, but they were not tender to the flowers and trees in their defense, and left many trampled and dead in the wake of their combat. The fomori blood oozed from ruptured bodies and spoiled the ground, wilting more of the growing life of the glade.

Ophelia wept, more distraught over the damage to the garden than about her own wounds. Devon sneered, and laughed at her. "Old woman, quit your crying. You can always buy more flowers. Such valor as we displayed here, however, comes not every day."

"Oh, you vain pup!" she cried. "Years it took for these plants to grow as they did, but now they are trampled and their spirits gone. The wisdom of all their ancestors' seeds lay dormant within them, but is now fled back to spirit realms too far for these old bones to search for. My life is worth less than this lore. Without it, how can your caern stay pure? Is there not a great and mighty tree in your caern? What if this were to sicken with disease — would not your caern's magic die with it?"

"You're speaking prattle, woman," Devon declared. "The Mighty Oak has ever been there and always shall remain. It was struck many lifetimes ago by Grandfather Thunder's lightning, and still bears the scar, a sign to us all of its holiness. What could survive such a bolt can easily withstand disease."

"Think you so?" Ophelia said. "One day it may come that the Oak will beg for the lore this garden once held, and then you will be obligated to search far and deep for it, and regret that you ever trampled so much as one stalk."

"Ha!" Devon said, gathering his pack to leave now that their work was done. "Then I will call on you to accompany us, should such an unlikely quest ever be called."

"And I will come, then," Ophelia said, and turned to the repair of the glade.

Years passed before her warning bore fruit, for she knew that if the fomori would be so bold as to attack her glade, they would also be aware of the Mighty Oak, and seek its downfall also. Through cunning and surprise, Banes did poison the ancient tree.

Wrought with anger and grief, the elders tried to summon spirits to aid and heal the tree, center of their caern's power. But no spirit knew how to heal such an old thing, but gave rumor that such lore existed deep in the Umbra, among spirits who had passed torn and wounded once a few years past, fleeing the assault on the Moon Glade.

Remembering the boastful tales of Devon Dark Brow and his mocking laughter of Ophelia the Gardener, the elders sought to punish him for the crime, and set a task before him that, should he refuse, would cost him greatly in renown.

His pride great before them, he took the quest to seek the lost plant spirits, and gathered his pack.

Down strange moon paths they went, hoping that Luna would aid them and lead them to their destination, but they were soon lost, for Luna resented their pride, and thought to teach them a lesson. After many misadventures in realms weird and bizarre, they came upon Ophelia, waiting for them at a crossroads.

"Are you ready to follow me now, Shadow Lord?" she asked.

"How did you find us?" Devon asked, unable to hide his surprise. "We have been lost for weeks!"

"The Lunes guided me. I asked kindly. Now, you said long ago that you would call on me if such a quest as yours arose. Your aimless wandering was punishment for ignoring that promise."

Chastened, Devon was quiet for a while, arguing with his rage. When he got the better of it, he calmed and spoke again: "Then accompany us you shall. But know that I lead this pack."

"Of course, but I am eldest, and you ignore my advice at your peril."

Devon growled but nodded, leading his pack onward. This time, the Moon Paths curved for them, rather than against as before, and led them soon to a green and verdant realm, a jungle teeming with plant spirits where their power was such that the animal spirits here lived only by their sufferance, rather than the reverse as it is in the material world.

Ophelia knew the proper decorum to display before these spirits, and only through her did they gain access deep into the realm. The trees and vines parted for them, but only after showing that they could just as easily entrap them if they so desired.

The spirits they sought had come here long ago, the local spirits claimed, seeking healing in the deepest glade where a shallow pool provided power to them. As the pack wandered for days seeking the pool, they saw signs that the realm was not as uncorrupted as they had at first thought, for black sap bled from some trees, and branches formed malignant shapes. Chases Foxes, the pack's Theurge, grew wary, and became convinced that Wyrm spirits hid from them, watching their passage.

Finally, they reached the pool, but found that it was not clear and cool as promised, but brackish and oily. "Something is terribly wrong here," Ophelia said. "A taint has come to this place."

"Then let's begone now, before it overcomes us," Devon said.

But it was too late. Huge bark-covered hands lashed out from the dark canopy, and grabbed each member of the pack. Only Ophelia slipped from the hard grasp as the other wolves were lifted into the air, struggling against the branches.

A dark rumble as of laughter filled the glade, and face appeared on the trunk of a tree. It spoke to them, oozing menace: "So, you have come for those you abandoned long ago. They are mine now, as are you. Do you not recognize me, Devon? For you carved your name into my trunk after your first rite!"

Devon growled, "You lie! Never have I seen such a vile thing as you!"

"Oh, but you have. I am the Mighty Oak who you sought to heal. Your aimless wandering kept you too long. I have passed into this realm, and made alliance with my new master, whom you shall soon meet…"

"Impossible!" Devon cried, too ashamed to raise his rage. "You cannot be that revered and ancient tree! Such a thing as old as it could never become corrupt so quickly!"

The wretched oak drew his branches in toward him, pulling the pack towards a hole in its side, a lightning-scarred wound that had never healed. But before it could stuff the Garou into the rent, green shoots wrapped around them, and tugged them back. The plant life from outside the glade had entered and now struggled with the Wyrm tree for ownership of the wolves.

As the spirits fought, and the Garou struggled to break their bonds, Ophelia climbed the oak and slipped into the rent in its bole, unnoticed by the warring tree. When inside, she withdrew her precious seed. She had hoped never to use it, for its power could not be recaptured. But the need was vital, and she knew what must be done.

Chanting a prayer, she breathed softly on the seed in her palm, and as she did, its spirit awoke and stretched outwards, breaking the shell, sending green shoots and flowering leaves in all directions.

When the Wyrm oak sensed what went on within its trunk, it roared in rage and released the Garou, concentrating instead on destroying the invaders. Ophelia scrambled to escape, but slowed by age, she was not quick enough. The hole sealed, trapping her and the newly-released spirit inside.

Devon recovered quickly and commanded his pack's assault. They swarmed about the tree's trunks and slashed at its roots, throwing their Crinos-weight against the bole, trying to uproot the thing. Other plant spirits aided them, and yanked at its branches, tugging to and fro to unbalance it. Their might yielded little, for the oak was old and rooted tight.

Then, to their surprise, its gray and crusty bark turned brown. Its dead branches grew leaves, and its struggles ceased. The lightning hole slowly opened, and flowers spilled out. An aroma powerful and sweet spread through the air, and even Devon could not suppress a smile at the joy of it. Nothing like it had ever been smelled before, and even the plant spirits swayed in celebration.

A shoot roamed outward and into Devon's face, and its petals opened, spilling dew onto his snout, and every wound within him, physical and spiritual, healed on the instant. Old hates and jealousies were gone, as were scars gained as a small child. Whole from head to toe he was.

"What is this?" he stammered. "How can this be?"

And then he saw Ophelia climbing from the hole, but she was bloody and broken. He rushed to catch her as she fell from the rent, and gently laid her on the greening loam.

She raised her eyes to him and smiled. "Ah, I see you have tasted its nectar."

"I don't understand," Devon said. "How did you do this wonderful thing?"

"I did nothing but hatch a seed, a very old seed. It is a flower that lay dormant since the Dawn, and only now sees the sun. Take a seed from its fruit back with you and plant it in the Moon Glade, so that its like will be seen on earth as well as in this realm."

"You will be the one to plant it," Devon said, fighting back tears.

Ophelia smiled. "One last journey will I make, but not on wolf feet. Good-bye, Shadow Lord." And she closed her eyes and died, and Devon let out a howl. Not a cry of rage but of sorrow, for he missed her in that moment more greatly than any loss in his life before.

They buried her body there, beneath the blossoming oak and Dawn flower, and marched sorrowfully home. They arrived to find the Mighty Oak well, and from the Umbra tiny blossoms of flowers could be seen on its branches, from the flower which wraps about its spirit elsewhere in the spirit realm.

And after telling the tale, and singing the praises of Ophelia Beloved-of-Moon, Devon went alone to the Moon Glade, and planted the seed he had brought. He went back often to tend it. After a while would rarely leave the place, for the other flowers and trees needed tending also, and there was no one else to take up the task.

After a time, when new packs returned from their rites of passage, they would pass the garden and laugh at the Shadow Lord who walked there, snickering that no Shadow Lord of any honor would waste time with plant spirits. But they would not tarry long, and Devon learned to ignore them.

Elders would come, and wise Garou from other lands, to view the garden and the Dawn Flower which grew there. And Devon would tell them the story of Ophelia and his own pride, and they would take it back with them to their moots, and tell the tale on cold nights when winter chilled their spirits and spring was most missed in the world.

Gibbous Moon: Sacrifice

There's a lot of misery to being a Garou. We all hope, though, that our suffering will help others. Sometimes, we even give our lives for others, or to stop the halt of the Wyrm. Always honor such sacrifice. Always. You never know when or if you will be called by Gaia to give everything to defend Her. Know that if you do, we will sing your songs, and remember.

The City of Maggots

In the old days, vampires raised cities filled with degenerate humans that worshipped them as gods. Every once in a while, we found them... and dealt with them in the appropriate fashion.

Breath of my fathers! Wash away the stench of death

That hangs across this land! For the walking dead have conspired

With their living slaves to construct a maggot-city

And to fill it with all the terrors of the night!

Oh, the Wyrm was in full-flower here!

With his coils and his lies he poisoned the earth.

Once, tall towers of black-etched stone rose like anger into the darkness,

And the soil was ripe with rotting carcasses

That not even a fly would touch!

Inside the walls, fountains flowed with the stolen blood of babes,

And plants flowered with green ichor and purple blossoms.

Such was the malaise upon the soil that Falcon himself

Descended from the clouds to cry for a cleansing!

And so we have gathered, from four tribes, we come:

Dol-ah-Shen, the Strider with savage eyes!

Isthsmene and Medusa, most brilliant Furies!

Grantor the Get, with bloody paws!

Iskeka the Fang, with snapping jaws!

I, Tehuti-ut-Tera, call forth the allies of our people
And cast strong gifts at the heart of the blight.
With our hosts and kin, we have swept the city bare!
Now it roars with cleansing flames.
We fought through the streets, those black-paved expanses
Of dust and bloodstains, to answer the call
Of Heru, the lord; of Falcon, our friend, to
Pull down the towers and wash away filth
Scattered here by the vampire lords.
Like wizened kings, these leeches ruled
The burning sands and trading-ports of
This city, crouched like a hunting-cat
On the bay of Reed-Flowers' Bend,
(Where long ago, old Sala held back 50 creatures
Of the Unmaker's brood!)
Defiled the battle-ground of our own bygone friend.
From cities and ports of disreputable kind,
Came worshipping throngs, to comfort the beasts!
Full-willing, they opened their veins to the lords,
And fed them on carnage and innocence wrecked.
Like flies on the limbs of the Eater-of-Souls
These corrupted mortals gave over their wills to
The wretched excess of the vampire-kings
Till the whole land was poisoned by unholy things.
Oh, Falcon! See what we have done!
Oh, Heru, see your will come to pass!

With the gifts you have laid at our feet, we have
Dragged down the palace of pestilence.
With the friends you have sent us, we have
Punished the spawn of the Wyrm.
It was bitter and hard, this challenge of fire,
Far too many heroes have been laid to the pyre.
Dol-ah-Shen, my brave lord, has been rent by the might
Of two-score howling creatures of night.
Half-buried in corpses, he stood until blood flowed from fifty-score wounds;
Until his arms were wrenched out of their sockets and burned.
Still, his jaws snapped out at the fray,
Snatching gobbets of flesh from the screaming death-hordes!
Oh, ancestors, welcome him!
Oh, my fathers, bear him away with your sighs!
Grantor fought well, but was bathed in acid spilled
From the black-palace walls of one foul reside.
As his flesh bubbled away from his bones, he
Swept like a demon across the onrushing hordes!
Not once did I hear him cry out, so filled was
His gullet with befouled gore! When he fell
The capering beasts screamed and fled, their hands burning
From the touch of his still-seething flesh!
Oh, Mother, welcome him!
Fenris, bear him to your side!
Isthsmene leapt upon the backs of two great monstrosities,
Twelve-handed giants shaped by fell sorceries.
Her claws reaped deep furrows in the flesh of these things,
But as they died, they crushed her beneath their great feet!
Oh, spirits, welcome her!
Oh, Mother, return her to your womb!

Many others died, also: sweet Helena, fair Nesro,
Brave Quin-ta-Na, cold Hylus, gentle Clyta, huge Gryvind,
Iksthos the Wise, Bardi the Bold, Ryvinna the Chaste
    and Hajjra the Kind.
Three cat-changers, too, fought by our side:
Ay survived, but Merikare was crushed by great hammers,
And Clothos was flayed
By a vampire lord with four mighty blades!
Ancestors, honor them all!
Luna and Gaia, regard them with pride!
Most shameful is one I will not name,
Whose claws were turned against his own kind.
Let him lie without mourning, let his skin be unburned!
If the spirits wish to comfort him, let them do so
Without our favor or call!
And another, whose name is likewise abhorred,
Abomination, let her be named!
For she has been taken by the leeches of night,
And has been turned into one of their own!
May her spirit wither from shame!
Let her bones blacken beneath the healing sun!
Oh, ancestors, renounce them!
Oh, my kin, let their names be forgot!
Our losses are grave, yet the towers still burn.
Let the ashes of leeches be left to the sun!
Let the salt be cast down where towers once stood,
Let the Rites of Purgation drive the Wyrm from this land!
For we are victorious!
For we have triumphed!
For they have fallen!
And all is done.

A Mother's Lament

Is this a lament by a Garou mother after the death of her child? Or a pack leader sized by Harano? Or is it the Earth, whose children have all perished... or worse yet, have been disowned for their selfishness? Perhaps even Gaia after the Apocalypse, grieving for the "three embers" she once birthed? I do not know — I can only sing the tale that I was given.

A single cloud in an empty sky
Once full, now falling, bit by bit.
Empty, barren, nothing can grow
That has been felled like dead wood
Or burned like summer grass.
Empty, sterile, barren as stone.
Empty, barren as the dust.
To know this broken tree or field
Can grow again is
No comfort.
No comfort.
The sky is empty.
The rain has fallen.
And still nothing lives.
Nothing grows again.
And I fall, bit by bit
Like rain into the dust.

Full Moon: Valor

I sing of the blood we spill from our own veins, of the quaking limbs and thundering hearts that we still when we meet the enemy claw-to-claw. I invoke the spirits of War and Courage, the totems of protection and ferocity and most of all of remembrance. For valor demands sacrifice too, and no battle worth winning is gained without first fighting down the demons of terror and loss.

The Fall of the False Prince

Leadership is vital. A strong arm is only good when the mind that wields it is keen and sensible. One of the biggest problems we've had across the ages is poor leadership — and by that, I don't mean to insult the Silver Fangs alone. Many a pack has been led into disaster by an Alpha who wasn't of the 'Fangs, and many a good Fang has taken his (or her) pack through the darkness and into dawn.

Lord Alexsei Yevgenvich stands as a testament to wise leadership. When many of his kinsmen were literally at each other's throats, he gathered up a Silver Pack and hunted down the nests of magi, Leeches, demons, deceivers and rival wolves who plagued the Russian night. Lord Alexsei provides a model of fairness long after his demise.

This tale has an interesting history, which I won't bore you with here. Suffice it to say that part of the original tale was lost, but with the aid of spirits, it has been restored somewhat. The presence of more than one author still tells, however.

Into the Dragon's Castle they went for Mother Russia: Lord Alexsei Yevgenvich of the Silver Fangs, his brothers Varya and Konstantine, Sees-at-Night the Talon, Sergiev of the Get, Varvara the Shadow Mistress and Illyania the Fury, whose eyes shone red as hot coals. Four times had the false prince Dmitrii risen to bleed the people dry; three times had he been set to rest, only to return. This final time, a Silver Pack assembled in the howling hills. After gutting his regime and throating their enemies, these worthies found the Dragon's tail. Biting it, they chased the false prince into the wastes, then followed to his lair.

Now the wind rose high on an icy steppe, freezing warm fur into briars. Still the army of Alexsei, ever-grim, advanced on their quarry. Far off, perched on an overhang, sat the Castle Trigorin — artifact of the days when the Tatar Horde bore across the land. Not so long before, old Ivan had used that place as a garrison for atrocities, and still the land bore the Dragon's stamp. From the Southern mountains, a secret Wyrm-led order had raised the very stones of Castle Trigorin. This Order of the Dragon had pledged to aid the Holy Church, but as any pup well knew it sheltered blasphemies instead, and fed the Wyrm warm suppers on cold nights.

It was the plan of Lord Alexsei to reach the Castle by daylight. In the cleansing rays, the charnel horrors of that house would cower in the catacombs for fear. But the weather was against them, and the wind beat them down, and the mountains shook with the falling snows. The spirit-Gifts allowed the Pack to make its way where none other could, but by the time they gained the castle road, the winter light was fading. Darkness was at hand!

As the sunset turned the clouds to embers, Lord Alexsei gathered counsel. Should they wait till break of day, or would the native cunning of the prince in his own lands grant them disadvantage? "Strike now!" urged Sees-at-Night. Illyania agreed. Like the Leeches, these two could see through Hell itself. "If we wait," the Fury said, "we will be taken unawares by them that know this place." Varvara and the Get concurred, but Varya and Konstantine held back. "In the night, these things are strongest," they maintained. "To go against them now is to chase a fish below the ice." Sergiev called them coward, but the brothers held fast. Their furs bristling, they stood back-to-back, daring the rest of the Pack to throat them.

"Enough of this!" Lord Alexsei commanded, going against his brothers' wishes. "It is decided. We shall enter the Castle by full moonlight, but first we shall prepare a bundle of stakes and other tricks with which to baffle the Prince's leamen." So saying, he turned to Varvara the Ragabash. "See to your deceptions," he told his packmate. "For the Dragon is blind to jests."

"And see to your weapons," the Lord told his brother Konstantine the blades-master. "For the silver of your klaives is proof against their magics and shall see us through the bitter night."

"And see to your songs of power," he told the Fury, "for the ears of the Damned cannot abide such music. When our strength falters, I know you will be there beside us. As your notes carve the flesh from our foemens' bones, you will sustain us in our rage."

"And see to your vision, friend," he told Sees-By-Night, "for we shall all rely upon your keen sight and senses. With you by our side, no demon can elude us. I am glad to have you as my packmate!"

"And see to your strength, good brother," he told Sergiev, "for like the Fenris you are named for, your howls affright the horses of Hell themselves! Glad am I to call you my right hand, and well do I trust your might."

"And see to your companions," he told his brother Varya (also called "the Mad"), "for with your eyes to the spirit-world, we shall not be alone. Those allies shall bear us through this trial and see us safely home, even if we fall tonight."

And together they hailed him, for his wisdom was great. As the cold raged down like a curse, the Silver Pack entered the barren lands of the false prince.

Through the winding wooded paths to the Castle they padded, as wolves in form, hunters in intent. Close to the walls they came with no sign of living being. The night was too cold to host even birdsong, although whether wings would alight on these dread branches all the pack had doubt.

Sergiev lead the way, but all were halted by Varvara's whimpered whine. To the stones of the rising outcrop she hung close, and by her noise called the others to her, revealing cave under rock, leading into darkness deep below the Castle. In grunting wolf-tongue they argued again, on course of entry: through

Castle gates bold and strong or through caverns dark, slinking in pits unseen and unsuspected?

Again Alexsei broke the arguing growls, and bid Sees-At-Night to enter the dank cave, and others followed, resolved now under leader's claim. Through tight holes and dripping stone they clambered, sniffing ahead for sign of foe or trap. Only bats awaited their coming, but clung to hanging perch, unafraid of wolves that passed.

With keen eye and keener nose, the Talon led the pack to foundation of stone, to a door bolted fast into carved rock. Shifting forms to battle-stance, Konstantine and Sergei greeted the door with shoulders broad, and cracked it before their bulks. Splintered and undone, the door opened to winding stairs leading up to Castle proper. Sergei again led, his might prepared to face whatever waited in above foyer.

Into empty hall they came, with the soft whisper of flesh on flesh the only voice. Curtains and hangings lined the hall, shifting restlessly in unseen and unfelt wind. Living things they were, flesh sheets molded from mortals, those who had displeased the lord of the manor. Silent screams their faces attempted, but no sound so shrill could they emit.

Illyania's rage overcame her will and with claws she slashed at the Leech's victims, whose relief played on faces flat to curtained wall. Blood sprayed across the stones as rent asunder were the sheets, and still no scream could they cry as slowly, painfully they died.

As the last of such morbid art gave up its ghost, candelabra near lit with unholy light, revealing the unwelcome guests. Konstantine did not wait for cue, he rushed to the ballroom at end of hall, and there gave announcement of his arrival with chilling howl.

Inside that damned room there writhed all the handicrafts of the house: tables, chairs, divans and dishwares, leaping and sliding across the marble to assault the wolf. Not of metal or wood were these things wrought, but like the curtains of flesh with veins purple and vile. Animate with anger and hate, these puppets were played with invisible strings, attached to the hand of the Prince Dmitrii.

On a throne he sat and orchestrated his servants, bored and expectant for entertainment. Teeth its handicrafts revealed, and bit into Konstantine's flesh, sucking his life in great gulps.

A great wind from the passage blew them away, scattering them across the room and away from their prey. Illyana stepped in, battle-form, her visage grim. The rest of the pack followed her lead, and spread across the room, stalking the pretender on the throne.

Tired of his game, the great vampire shed his skin, and revealed that he was more pretender than they had known, for no undead lord was he, for dragon scales glinted in bale candle light, guttering flames sparking green and sickly on his reptilian skin.

Alexsei cried to his pack: "Beware, he is Zmei-kin, a Wyrm-beast! My brothers, defend the others, as I wrestle the dragon."

"No, Alexsei," Konstantine said, his wounds still bleeding, "Do not steal from us this glory!"

"Fool!" Alexsei cried, "I go forth to die! You shall stay behind, and tend the pack in my stead." With that, he charged forward, and bit down upon the serpent Prince, now inhuman in all appearance. As they tossed and fought on the flags, the very walls became alive, and Banes birthed in sickly swamps rose up to drown the pack.

Alexsei's brothers only then saw the wisdom of their leader. As they defended their pack brothers, it took everyone's strength to win a retreat, for too great by far were the besetting beasts.

Alexsei howled in anguish as his wounds grew greater, but Dmitrii too cried as his blood spread forth to stain the floors. Finally, after trading blows uncounted, both died wrapped in anger, their spirits unchained by the others' fierce hate.

With the passing of the dragon, the charms went from the Castle, freeing Banes from hard-won bindings. They fled their captivity, a more desired thing than the death of their enemies.

The pack gathered about their fallen leader, and howled in anguish at their loss. Lord Alexsei's bravery and leadership was sung that night, at moot fire under moon bright. All the Motherland did weep, to hear the tale of sacrifice deep.

And ever from that day, his brothers their respect paid, honoring always Alexsei's wisdom, to plot for victory even over pride of kin.

Eclipse: Shame

There is no honor without betrayal, no valor without treachery. I sing now of those-who-will-not-be-named, of Garou whose deeds have been so infested with shame that we have preserved their tales — but not their names — to serve as lessons of what we must not be. Listen and remember!

Lament of the First Ronin

This tale, centuries old, is certainly apocryphal. No one has ever spoken to the this legendary monster long enough to have heard what it thinks about anything in particular, much less to have gained its sympathy. Like the Satanic verses of Lord Byron and Baudelaire, and the corpse poetry of the Renaissance, this Lament is the work of some Galliard who wanted to get inside the head of a powerful adversary and reflect the ties we have to him. As such, I think it's far more powerful than the tales that simply tell us that the First Ronin is a bad guy. Here, he assumes a tragic aspect that seems all the worse considering what he'll probably do to you if you actually try to have a conversation with him. "Sympathy for the Devil," for sure!

Cursed be those who bore me! I vomit

Tempests upon the two whose shameful lay

Brought down the ax of hate and birthed in me monstrosity!

Cursed be he whose burning paws

Swept tears from my Dam and transformed

Her protestations to a bawd;

Cursed be she whose bower-womb clutched

At him even as the skies opened like her legs in shame!

For I am a dissonance, abomination

To the ranks of your pure majesties.

I howl plagues upon the waves of all

The seas that nurture you, and

Spit my spite into the sun.

Night is to me what love was to your kind;

O purposeful concealer and party to my thirst!

Let the wombs of all innocents be split like

The hare whose race has failed

And whose bones crack with its final spasm-kicks,

Let their blood be my repast.

I was driven to the night with whips

63

And kisses of sweet silver flame
Cursed be you whose righteousness has set my name alone,
Cursed be this white hide, its burning glyphs and prophecies,
And fie upon the skin of night that ever shelters me.
Beg me as I might for death, this world
Has need of me, it seems,
For she shall not take leave of me,
Until — at last! — her dreams
Fall cold as stones upon the land.
While the worms send your spirit to the sky,
Mine dances, eternal destiny
Where none might bring surcease.
No waters shall drown these dusty truths,
So take comfort in your fall.
Were I you, I would
Enjoy the sleep.
I cannot, and so I burn.

A Call to Rage

One of the greatest crimes imaginable is fratricide. Yet, long ago we killed our cousins out of turn, slaughtered them to the brink of extinction as if we were the humans we so deeply resent. It's been millennia, but the bloody slash of those days has barely scabbed over. Every so often, we pick at it. Why did our forebears — why did we — do such a thing? What was it that caused "the Flood of Scarlet Sorrow," the so-called "War of Rage" that set us eternally at odds with the other Changers?

Who the hell knows? Some Galliards still make up excuses for the War, as if justifying a sibling's murder might somehow make the whole thing okay. Most just refuse to talk about it at all, as if by ignoring the War, they could pretend it didn't happen. Well, it did happen, and our nights are poorer for it. Maybe, when we stand across the field from the Wyrm's last army, we'll wish we had more of our Changing cousins at our backs.

And maybe, if we take a look at the prejudice and misconceptions — or even truths of nature — that sparked the War, we might be able to muster up a good defense when the final battle starts.

There are many tales of the War, but very few that come from the beginning. I heard this one through the ears of a past-life, around a bonfire that reached into the sky. As the Silver Fang who spoke it raised the cry, he held up skulls from slaughtered enemies. As he read the names of the other breeds, he raked his claws across the glyphs that stood for the different Changers, wet his claws in his own bloody chest, then recited the words again. It was pretty damned impressive, I'll give him that.

I'm not going to tell you what I remember after the moot. But it gives me nightmares, even now.

When the bodies of the dead fall to the hollowed ground
Raven comes on rattling wings to steal their eyes
And mock at us as he swallows their spirits,
Picking bones as prizes to his fear.
When the cold winds whip us from the shelter of the trees,
Bear drives us from her cave, devouring our offspring,
With her greedy paws, she makes a place for her young ones
While devouring our own to feed her hunger.
When the Coiled One whispers his enigmatic plans,
Cat is there with open ears and slashing talons
To keep such news from us, and she watches us
With eyes like crescent moons.
We must answer this with anger!
We must answer it with blood!
When we stumble into hidden places,
Dragon-King makes meat of us, and splays
Our questing legs like straw upon his dung-heap,
Our heads upon the ground like stones.
When misfortune roars like an angry Bane,

Bat chuckles from on high, and spreads tales;
For his chatter, we are driven down,
By his trickery, we are flayed alive.
When pestilence fells the strongest of our kind
And the bones of proud warriors rot with sickness,
Rat is there, with his mangy hide and
His bellyful of poisoned secrets.
Brothers and sisters, you know this is true!
Brothers and sisters, you know I speak the truth!
When from the tall grass, a
Sudden strike of fangs and crippling pain awakes,
Serpent is there, with her eternal gaze,
Her never-blinking eyes.
When webs of treachery and subtle guile
Trap us like an errant fly,
Spider prances across her spin-work
Like a Weaver made of night, she drains us into husks.
When poison bubbles below the earth,
Boar slices open the Mother's skin,
Releasing the venom into the forests,
Poisoning the beasts and the trees from his spite!
My kin, I know you know this truth!
My kin, I call upon you now!
Bite deep upon the flanks of errant cousins!
Reclaim our birthright in a storm of blood!
The Mother Moon is high and full,
Let our War of Rage begin!

The Raven's Warning

The legacy of the War of Rage haunts all Changers, even now. This fragment, part of a longer poem called "Eyes of the Soul," reflects the impression we give our cousins — cousins who sometimes make no distinction between ourselves and the things we hunt.

Fat yourself on the kill, good brother, but beware.

For the gratitude of wolves is fleeting;

that of men, more so.

Our cousins are too much of each, I fear,

And too hungry to care for giving thanks.

So when you fly to give them warning of the foul things below,

Take care not to let them catch you

Feasting on the eyes of their own fallen ones.

For if they could but see what we do in the shadows of night,

They would gut us, kin or no, for our presumption,

As once they did before.

Gifts

Anyone who has ever walked through a quiet wood, only to encounter a secret dumping ground can probably relate to this plaintive poem. It's not old — how could it be? — but I felt it was worth putting in the Record, if only to remind us how ungrateful we can be.

Beneath a blue sky, I saw ruins.

Beneath a blue sky I was ruined.

Glass and stone and metal and wood.

And no birdsong, only flies.

A lost corner, no one visits.

No one cares to clean the bones away.

Beneath the ruins, I am smothered.

Beneath the ruins, my bones are buried.

Air and trees and life and fire.

These are gifts I gave you freely.

Now glass glitters where the ivy grew.

And your gratitude is the sound of flies.

Bright Moon: The New

King Albrecht's Crusade Against the Seventh Generation

This is a new tale, entered barely a moon ago. You see, the Record isn't static — it's always growing. With each new moment of valor or honor, with each mighty deed, the Record increases. Maybe even you will one day do something so great that the spirits will come running to the keeper of the Record and demand a new entry in the saga of our tribes. I hope so. We need as many examples today as we can get.

Everyone knows — or should know by now — the tale of Lord Albrecht's winning of the Silver Crown and the throne of the Silver Fang North Country Protectorate. It's also part of the Record; I just didn't repeat it here. Instead, this tale is about his deeds after putting on the crown. Most leaders these days seem content to sit at the caern and send out the kids to do all the fighting. Not Albrecht. He's in the fray with the rest of them. Not only that, but he's trying to achieve something by raising awareness of a deeper danger than any of us have yet suspected.

Well, I'll let the tale tell all. It's written in rather a high style for modern times, but hey, that's what the Silver Fang Galliards of North Country are all about these days. It's an expression of their newfound purpose, so I figure it's okay. It does provide a certain link between the deeds of today and those of yesteryear — which is what the Record is all about, after all.

I just hope it does more than entertain. I hope it makes you get up and do something about the ills of the world.

I was there.

I was there to witness King Albrecht's slaying of the demon Draggerunter and the Wyrm's invisible minions.

I rallied at his call to battle an enemy none believed existed, and I swore before my thrice-bloodied klaive to follow him in his crusade no matter the odds against us or the guile of our enemies. I did the same for his grandfather, Morningkill. I do so for him. It is the Silver Fang way. When our king calls, we follow, no matter the madness that drives him.

But our new king is not mad. He sees into the invisible aethers cloaking the Enemy, and rightly identifies Banes haunting and gibbering just beyond the Veil of Shadow. And when he bids us attack, attack we do, with claw and fang and unsheathed klaive of sharpened silver.

I sing now of the courage of Albrecht, and the wisdom of his allies. His pack is mighty in all the virtues. Who are they? I sing their names:

Wise Evan Heals-the-Past, of ancient blood and young ways, child of Wendigo and Half-Moon;

Strong Mari Cabrah, whom none dare naysay without risk of battle scar, child of Pegasus and crescent moon;

Wise Antonine Teardrop, watcher of forgotten doors and paths, child of Chimera and Half-Moon;

Stalwart Loba Carcassone, defender of the defenseless, nurturer of lost cubs, child of Falcon and crescent moon.

Five strong, a circle bound by silver crown!

When did it begin? I will tell the tale:

The silver crown won through hard trial and threat of doom, King Albrecht set to make right the wrongs of the generation before him. He summoned allies to the North Country Protectorate, and made alliances with skeptical tribes long spurned by elder king. But no ruler to sit on laurels was he, for Albrecht went to those who would not come, and bade them parley, winning through earnest words what ancient authority could no longer sway.

The Uktena did he make pact with, and even the Wendigo. The Get and the Furies, all assented to his rule. Even the Shadow Lords yielded to his cause, when Grandfather Thunder rumbled his respect for the new king. Not easily won was the storm totem, but Umbral quest and bold foray into Wyrmdom lightened even dark Thunder's heart, and the Shadow Lords, humbled, opened ear to the Silver Fang (although gave no word of consent to spoil their pride!).

To these tribes again under one rule, along with the others who had never broke with Falcon's tribe, Albrecht made known his great intent, his long-growing purpose.

To the court he called Loba, long denied presence in it, and raised her to glory and wisdom, and much honor he put upon her in the sight of all. Abashed, she grew quiet, but then angry, for renown she did not seek, only surcease to the Wyrm's dark plots, now known to all.

Of her long battle against the Wyrm's most insidious minions all were told, and of her shepherding of wounded children all were appraised. A threat nigh unbelievable was revealed, long whispered but long spurned in idle talk: a hidden cabal with tentacles deep set in the hearts of man and child.

Of the Seventh Generation we were made aware. Of the Pentarch were we afeared, and its leaders disguised as mortals in all chapters of human endeavor. Of Loba's knowledge of them and the deaf ears we had turned to her cries for so long, we were ashamed. No more would this evil hide. Now would light be turned upon it, and its minions hunted in the night and days to come.

Not a single task was set before us, but many tasks, the winning of which would take many years. An evil so long hidden and grown like black fungus in the dark could not be killed in one night.

What was this evil? How did it differ from the greedy or the hungry servitors that escaped the Umbra to threaten the earth? Why was this threat greater than any before? It ate at the very core of Gaia in a way unlike any other Wyrm thing, for the Seventh Generation devoured our children and yet left them whole, with gnawed pits in their hearts which spread corruption unseen as years pass. Years upon years of abuse did they heap upon the young, not with their own hands, but through the hands of parents — wounded children themselves a generation before. An inheritance of hate they sowed, and ensured with each brood that the new was tainted by the old. So deep are the scars carved in childhood that those who grow to adulthood without succor and love cannot escape erecting dread chimares of their dreams, ever haunting them and causing them to taint all they touch.

Such was the wisdom of our new king that his crusade was not to be fought with might alone. Only healing could assuage the future taint, so rites of brotherhood and warding were declared. No victim of the Wyrm would be abandoned in the wake of this war — healing would be had for all.

But how to work such a hospice? And here the unity of Gaia's purpose in her 13 tribes showed through, for not all of us were made for war or wisdom; some were made to nurture and heal, and succor the wounds caused by the Wyrm. And here we were shamed, for all realized that for too long were songs of war sung when wounds needed healing. Compassion was Gaia's way also, and her Children had never forgotten this.

Not only the Silver Fangs share in this crusade, but all Garou of all tribes. The packs of cubs new from their first rites joined in, clamoring for glory and the king's eye that day.

And so the quests began, to send the packs out to seek knowledge of our enemy, to track down its incognito soldiers and identify them to all. Once done, battles would be planned, assaults to move quickly and cleanly against the unsuspecting foe. Oh how many moons it took before blood was shed! Hard to find the evil was, and only Umbral eyes could finally see it through its shell of concealment, hidden in the souls of those who serve it. But the battles did come, on many fronts, and many were the Banes to die screaming under Garou claw. Many more were the humans who died, too stupid to know whom they served.

Battle scars we bled, and still did some doubt our crusade and the existence of our enemy. They denied the conspiracy that linked our prey, and claimed it was but coincidence, that the Wyrm was many but certainly not clever.

But packs traveled far and witnessed much now that their eyes were opened by Loba, and proof after proof did arrive that a web of well-planned workings ensnared our seemingly disconnected prey. Even the doubters shut their snouts, and bowed their heads to Albrecht's rule, united as never before to squash this foe.

To prove before all Garou the evil that had plotted through generations, Albrecht gathered his pack, and went himself with them to war. Careful intelligence and the spies of many packs had finally uncovered a powerful servant of the Pentarch. His death would be a warning to the others that we knew of them and that their work was through. Once exposed, they could no longer work in secret, and their powers would wither.

Albrecht gathered his war party, choosing the best among us, and I was honored to stand among them.

Along secret moon paths revealed only to the king we traveled, beguiled by Lunes so that we could not follow the paths again without Albrecht's lead, and finally we came upon the Umbral lair that hovered about our mortal foe.

We silently stalked from our secret paths and waylaid the Banes that swam in those murky Airts, spilling their ichor before they could let loose cry to their allies. In silence, we drew ever closer, circling our enemy in a trap so tight none could flee without encountering a waiting pack.

Peering into the material world, we espied our prey, the fatted lamb full of bloated and stinking blood. He sat in his mansion content with his work, for that very day he had thrown humans off the trail of his evil, convincing them that memories of abuse awakened in child were mere fantasies. A mind-doctor he was, hailed by humans as a font of wisdom on the workings of human minds. Yet he only used this lore to corrupt such minds.

Sipping his vile bever, he could not suspect that a king of the Silver Fangs stared at him from the Umbra, and yet some chill wind on his spine alerted him to danger. He peered about, using his magics to see into our hiding place, whereupon he cried in shock and fear. A growl escaped King Albrecht's lips as he shifted into Crinos and stepped through the Shadow into the material world to greet the demon called Gunter Draggerunter.

The bloated mortal stumbled back in fear, recognizing the Garou before him for a mighty hero, but he did not forego his own defense, for he snapped his cane in twain, freeing the monster which slithered within its confines.

Swirling in rings of smoke the Bane wrapped about King Albrecht and squeezed him tight, its poison seeping into this skin. Never had we seen such a thing, for the Bane worked quickly and resisted Albrecht's might. Antonine Teardrop knew it and called its name: Ichorous Urge, a spirit of the Defiler Wyrm's own poison venom. The pack stepped forward from the Shadow as one, and engaged the creature's coils.

We prepared to follow but were beset ourselves by coils of smoke and poison — the thing was both in Spirit and in matter! Only I and his packmates reached the material world before realizing my comrades' danger — too late, as I engaged our king's foe.

Heals-the-Past, Wendigo warrior, summoned the ice which chilled the room, and slowed the serpent in its writhing, so that Mari's furious claws could fly true and straight, and sever its scales from its skin. The coils loosed by ice and claw, Albrecht burst them from himself and a howl of rage escaped his maw.

Draggerunter ran from the room, and Albrecht followed in a storm. While his pack clawed and slashed as the remaining tentacles — writhing and alive even when split — the king chased the demon. I followed, fearful for my liege.

Yet I had no cause for fear. Mighty is Albrecht, mightier even than all his friends know. He shifted to Lupus and nipped at the demon's heels, slicing his meat from his bones so that the monster fell upon the floor, crashing in a mighty heap. Draggerunter whimpered, unable to retaliate against such a force. He evaded enemies through cunning, not brawn. Weak were his limbs before the Garou!

Albrecht raised his grand klaive and brought it down on the vast flesh that hid the demon's neck from view. Bone and flesh severed, and the evil doctor's head rolled across the carpet, spilling its black blood.

With Draggerunter's death, the Ichorous Urge disappeared, summoned back to the dark courts where was its lair. We knew it would report its defeat to its masters, and were proud that they would tremble in anger and shame at their loss.

We burned that mansion to the ground, and made rites upon it to cleanse its grounds, and to root out any evil still hiding there, and set guard upon the place lest evil return.

A great moot was held to survey the spoils of that night, and many Banes were counted dead, and very few of our number had fallen. Those that did were sung songs of valor, and we begged our ancestors to look after their spirits in the world that awaited them.

Who now can deny that the Seventh Generation minions are spawned from the deepest Wyrm pit? Who else but they can summon the rarest Banes to aid them?

Antonine spoke to all and bid them seal their lips outside of consecrated moot, for our enemy would now have eyes and ears and other senses besides searching for us and any sign of our next assault. We will adopt their secrecy to war against them, and strike where least expected, at secrets our foe thinks are well defended.

And then spoke Albrecht, rising before the packs assembled, and bid them this:

"Get out there and find out what's going on. I want to know who's who and what they're up to. But keep it quiet. If you have to, use the more boisterous packs as decoys. The enemy will expect us to act stupid and noisy. Can you blame them? Don't pander to their expectations — find out their game plan and report back to the elders here. Then, and only then, will we kick some Wyrm ass."

So it is said! Let all who do not cower heed! Open eyes and nostrils and seek out scents of hidden taint, for not all masks are faces of fear, and some may lie in bowers of innocent heart, wrapped in silk of forgotten fear wrought full upon childhood spirit, ready to hatch into insects of chittering torment.

Root out the poison but forget not to heal the wound, lest it fester again and birth worse tumors. This our lesson be, that evil within is the greatest enemy.

Remember

Well, there's more, but the moon grows old and tired, and so do I. You'll hear the rest when the time is right, when you need them most. The spirits will know.

You've received a great treasure from them. Now you must repay it. Not in money or fetishes, of course, but in like kind. You carry with you your own stories of the things you have witnessed. Whenever one tale stands above all others, when its telling is bursting from your tongue, seek out other Garou and spirits with ears for hearing such things, and tell that tale. They will carry it in their hearts now, and by a fire on a night many moons distant from now, they'll tell it again, to fresh ears. So the saga spreads. Someday, it'll get back to me, and if it's worthy, I'll enter it onto these skins, so that it will never be lost.

But even should something happen to me or the Record, the spirits remember what we've done, even when all mortal Records have gone to dust. We are, in our honor and our shame, immortal. Never forget that, my brothers and sisters. Everything you do will be remembered.

The Language of Glyphs

The glyph language is the perfect vehicle for werewolf expression. The Garou carve their pictograms with their own claws, as befits creatures of Rage. The glyphs themselves are very flexible in meaning, and lend themselves to a multitude of interpretations, depending on their context — the same glyph might mean "Gaia" in one marking, or "alive" in another. Although this system seems unnecessarily simple, it lends itself well to both homid and lupus patterns of thought. No other writing can as readily convey the essence of what it is to be a werewolf — and more, what it is to be Garou.

Glyphs have power. Each claw-cut pictogram of the Garou has been invested with a portion of the language, and carries something of the spirit of its meaning. Indeed, many spirits have come to recognize the glyphs that represent them, sometimes even going as far as to respond as if summoned when presented with their namesake. Many fetishes are accordingly decorated with glyphs that pay homage to the spirit inside as a form of chiminage. Galliards and Theurges alike learn the pictogram language as quickly as possible; both auspices recognize the power in names, and their duty to use this advantage wisely.

One note of warning: The following explanation of what exactly glyphs are, and how one interprets them, isn't necessarily the sort of explanation new cubs get during their fostering. Most werewolves aren't even close to grammaticians, and circumvent this seeming problem by doing much of their explanations of the glyphs in the Garou language. Although some cubs find it hard to translate glyphspeak into a human tongue, it becomes much easier to understand the nuances when they approach it on a more intuitive level.

In other words, when assembling these elements yourself to produce phrases, warnings or even short epics, don't get too hung up on grammar or the "one true way" to put things together. The only thing that's really important is that it *looks* right — that's the only unbreakable rule for a visual language.

Legendry

Each tribe has its own story about how the Garou learned to use glyphs; since the werewolves have been carving their pictograms since virtually the Impergium, each explanation is equally plausible. The Silver Fangs claim that their Galliards devised the art during the first great battles against the Wyrm as a means of preserving the tales of glory. Conversely, the Get claim that Hrafn, the Raven, taught them the truth of power in symbolic marks, a power that they learned to harness as glyphs and as runes. The Uktena maintain that their tribe was responsible for the art of writing, as their occult searches regularly dealt with abstract and symbolic concepts that could not be depicted with simple sculptures; and as counterpoint the Silent Striders believe that pictograms evolved from their ancestors' trail-markings, although they don't loudly argue the point.

Perhaps the most incendiary claim comes from the Glass Walkers, who argue that writing was a human art that their ancestors, and eventually the other tribes, copied for themselves. This argument infuriates countless elders, who point to the human abandonment of symbols for abstract alphabets as proof of the humans' disconnection with their senses and visceral symbols.

Whatever the truth, there's no longer any way of proving it. No surviving Ancestor-spirit can claim that they were the first to use pictograms without first learning the language from another Garou, and even today the arguments continue.

The Medium

No matter the medium, the traditional way to inscribe a Garou glyph is with the Crinos claw. Not only is the claw an instrument that is always at hand, but a message carved into a tree or stone marks the author as clearly Garou. There can be no counterfeit this way; even the distinctly curved claws of the Bastet or the smaller claws of vampires, Ratkin or other creatures cannot easily duplicate the "hand" of a Garou-carved glyph. Ronin who have lost the wolf (and thus the ability to change shape) cannot carve glyphs in the proper fashion; neither can Kin. There are a few ways to forge it, but for the most part, only a werewolf can make the proper mark. And only a werewolf knows the proper mark to make.

Garou pictograms predate anything even close to modern writing surfaces; after all, it's commonly held that werewolves were passing written messages to one another even before humans figured out how to bake clay into tablets. The original writing surface was tree bark, making it easy to string together chips to form a story in physical form, whether worn as a necklace or handed from storyteller to storyteller. Although certainly a limited method of storing information, it worked well with the werewolves' oral traditions. Each pictogram served as a mnemonic, allowing the storyteller to recount what glorious deeds had been done and in which order.

Pictograms also serve neatly as territory markers. Many septs still to this day mark the boundaries of their bawn by carving glyphs into stone. Even some urban septs mark this practice, carving the appropriate pictograms into shadowed alleyways or cornerstones.

That said, even though the only traditional way to present a glyph is to carve it "by hand" into a proper surface, the last few centuries, particularly the 20th, have seen a few variations in medium. Uktena and Shadow Lords have been known to use blades rather than claws to carve glyphs, although they mainly do so to emphasize a point. A few Stargazers, Silent Striders and Uktena have used their claws and ink or blood to write on paper or hide; the Uktena have even bound magical effects into such papers, so that the power is released when the paper is burned. A few young Garou have learned the art of tattooing, and marked themselves and their packmates with appropriate badges; scar fetishes in the shapes of glyphs are even more common. A few Bone Gnawers have even been crass enough to spraypaint glyphs as boundary markers, although even *their* elders consider this disrespectful and dangerously "out in the open."

The Vocabulary

The glyph language has been all but unchanged since the First Times; when the humans moved from pictograms to complicated systems of alphabets or characters, the Garou glyphs remained as they always had. To this day, each glyph represents a rough concept, framed not in the sense of words or paragraphs, but rather a raw symbol.

This rather open-endedness can befuddle new-changed homid cubs, at least the literal ones. After all, to the novice, the language of glyphs can seem like a vocabulary composed entirely of sets of homonyms, without even the slightest hint of conjunctions, pronouns, tenses or any of the like. In short, it's apparently a mess.

However, this approach suits the Garou rather better than one might think. Werewolves rely on their full complement of senses, and aren't as visually oriented as humans; lupus in particular tend to think in terms of symbols and impressions, rather than thinking to themselves in the context of words. Similarly, the Garou have long supported an oral tradition, trusting each new generation of tale-tellers to interpret and tell their legends in a way immediately accessible to the audience at hand. Rather than get hung up over literal translations (like the Earth being created in seven days, because *that's what the book says*), they improvise and interpret their lore as they deem most appropriate.

Context is everything, though. Even the glyph that represents everything the werewolves fight for — the glyph for Gaia — can be read as "earth," "land," "country," "territory," "life," "peace" or several other concepts. It all depends on the surrounding elements. Thankfully, werewolves are rather used to this sort of thing. The Garou language itself is similarly light on "words" that mean specific things; a particular growl or whine might mean one thing if the speaker's body language is submissive, and another thing entirely if the speaker is tense and wary. As a result, werewolves tend to be rather interpretative and not so literal when conversing or carving or reading glyphs.

One subsection of glyph marks that isn't easily defined is the small one-stroke markings that convey an even greater variety of meaning, depending on the glyph in question. Their meaning is almost completely different from one glyph to the next, and even their shape varies. For instance, the small "children" marks on the Children of Gaia glyph, the thin mark over the "journey" element in the Silent Striders glyph, and the mad, thorny strokes in the Black Spiral Dancers glyph — all of these are variants of the same thing. These strokes are something like pronouns and something like punctuation marks; they are without meaning of their own, but accent and clarify the meaning of whatever elements they appear with. For want of a better word, these strokes are emphatics — they elaborate upon whatever symbols they appear in without adding entirely new concepts to the mix.

The Tribes

As something of an example of how concepts of separate elements fit together to form a common glyph, the following section looks at the pictograms of the tribes and their origins. In many cases the glyph chosen to represent a tribe came into being before the tribal name itself was chosen; needless to say, the glyphs shouldn't be taken as literal translations of the tribes' epithets. As with so many other things in the Garou world, symbolism is often more important than cold, hard definition.

Black Furies

The Furies, always werewolves of powerful convictions, chose an imagery of lightning and judgment. The "omega" symbol of their pictogram is, according to tribal legend, an image of a pair of scales. Fury tradition holds that the Greek letter omega was inspired by their own glyph, but the truth isn't known. In any event, it's apparent that the Furies are one of the tribes that chose their symbol first and their name second, if indeed their name wasn't given to them by other Garou.

Bone Gnawers

Although certain Galliards of other tribes have noted the Gnawer glyph's similarity to a scurrying insect, instead it's a very straightforward representation of a cracked bone between a wolf's fangs.

Children of Gaia

Perhaps the most straightforward of glyphs, this marker represents the patrons of all Garou, Luna and Gaia. The emphatics that in this case translate as "children" are carved to represent Garou standing tall and proud under the aegis of their creators.

Fianna

The Fianna glyph is emblematic of the tribe's reputation as bards and loremasters. Their glyph indicates a howl or song rising to Luna, and that sums up the Fianna rather neatly.

Get of Fenris

The Get of Fenris' glyph symbolizes the "wolf born of wolf"; in their case, direct descent from Great Fenris. A few younglings have commented on the glyph's similarity to the swastika, and wonder if, after centuries of the night-fear, certain humans didn't subconsciously associate the symbol with domination and strength. Most elders strike the offending philosophers with brutal speed and force for such a suggestion; sometimes they bother to add that the youngsters might try looking up just what the swastika meant before they start jumping to conclusions.

Glass Walkers

The Glass Walkers' mark has undergone plenty of evolution over the centuries. Originally, when the tribe still called themselves Warders, it was a simple glyph with only one horizontal cross-bar, representing a simple human house. As time passed and human buildings became more elaborate, the Warders eventually added a second cross-bar to represent the multi-story buildings that had become common. When the tribe began calling themselves the Iron Riders during the Industrial Revolution, a third bar was added (partly to symbolize railroad tracks as well as taller buildings). Finally, in the early 20th century, the

Glass Walkers took their current name, and amended their glyph to represent the skyscrapers of modern cities. In all cases, the emphatic is present to represent "those who walk among human places" instead of the places themselves.

Red Talons

When the Talons became a tribe, they chose to represent themselves with a simple glyph, easily drawn even in Hispo. Their glyph is emblematic of the tribe's primal side and connection with their Rage. The tribal name of "Red Talons" came later, and one myth holds that it was coined by a horrified Fianna who observed a Talon attack, *very* red in tooth and claw. The Talons didn't object to his characterization.

Shadow Lords

The Lords' glyph represents not so much an object as an action — it's carved by making a clutching motion with both claws. As such, it's representative of the Lords' tendency to conduct their affairs with an iron fist. However, long years of association have also brought that same element into the glyph language as the symbol for "shadow." The emphatics above this motion likely originally meant "those who seize and hold," but nowadays most werewolves read them as "those who own/master the shadows."

Silent Striders

The Striders identify themselves with the glyph for "journey," with an added emphatic to represent the tribe members themselves. This element is carved thin and close to the contours of the "road," emphasizing subtle, silent passage.

Silver Fangs

The glyph for the ruling tribe is based on an element with a dual meaning: both "destructive" and "silver." The two marks enclosing the center element are indicative of rank, not unlike a crown; the Fangs also use this motif to denote nobility when carving the pictograms for their various noble houses.

Stargazers

The Stargazers' pictogram is self-explanatory—a glyph for "star," somewhat elaborated upon in order to convey added importance and meaning. This refers to the Stargazers' penchant for astrology, true; but it is also a near-koan for the hidden meaning intrinsic to all things. Stargazer cubs are often advised to meditate on the symbol, in order to reflect on how the pictogram's lesson applies to all things.

Uktena

The Uktena glyph is somewhat confusing even to other Garou. Although it clearly contains the elements that imply "rite," the central combination of claw strokes doesn't appear anywhere else in the greater body of werewolf glyphs. Most presume that it's some sort of mystic symbol with a connotation known only to the Uktena themselves. The Uktena, of course, keep the secret for themselves.

Wendigo

The Wendigo's glyph symbolizes the wind across the face of the moon. It's essentially a metaphor for the cold northern nights that represent what it is to be Wendigo to the core — harsh and unyielding, but still with sufficient grace and beauty.

Croatan

The tribes of the Pure Ones each chose to identify themselves with their totems. In the Uktena and Wendigo's case, this meant taking the name of their totem as the name of their tribe. For the Croatan, it meant using the glyph of their totem, Turtle, to represent themselves.

Bunyip

The Bunyip didn't use any one particular glyph for themselves during most of their history. Upon initial contact with their European cousins, they settled on a common glyph meaning their homeland and personal territory — a glyph combining the element of "land" with the mark of their totem, Rainbow Serpent.

White Howlers

The White Howlers were a simple tribe, and their glyph was equally simple. Like their cousins, the Fianna, the Howlers identified themselves with the symbol for "howl" — but where the Fianna chose to stress the song aspect, the Howlers added emphatics of a slashing, rending, violent connotation to emphasize their warlike, berserker nature.

Black Spiral Dancers

The Dancers, alone among the tribes, didn't choose their tribal glyph. For some time after their fall, legend has it, the only use they had for pictogram writing was clawing madly at the walls. During that time, the Gaian Garou who first learned that an entire tribe had fallen to the Wyrm were horrified by the thought. To represent the horror, madness and corruption that the Dancers represented, they took the glyph for the Wyrm and added a host of frenzied, mad emphatics. As a result, the Black Spiral Dancers' glyph is almost painful to look upon — neatly conveying how their Gaian cousins feel about them. And with the demented practicality common to the Wyrm-wolves, the Dancers gleefully adopted this mark of horror and insanity as their own.

The Elements

The following is a brief glossary of the more common elements in the glyph language. Although it may seem horribly incomplete, remember that Garou tend to take the very direct route when carving pictograms. There's no need to say "deer" when "prey beast" will suffice; the person telling the tale is expected to remember the specifics, or interpret the story as suits the audience. (And Galliards have excellent memories; certainly one of the advantages a culture rich in oral history has over a culture dependent on soundbites and factoids.) There's no need for prepositions, conjunctions, or most of the other grammatical traditions — the glyph language relies more on gut impressions than it does on sentence structure.

Feel free to be creative when combining glyphs as you need to. Most of the common glyphs in use today are remarkably simple combinations of previously existing glyphs — take the glyph for "fomor," for instance. It's much easier than it looks.

The Garou

Garou, werewolf

Homid, human

Metis

Lupus, wolf

Ragabash, new moon

Theurge, crescent moon

Philodox, half moon

Galliard, gibbous moon

Ahroun, full moon

The Ways

Caern

Moot

The Litany

Pack, group, circle, alliance

Garou Nation

Rage, frenzy

Gnosis

Glory

Honor

Wisdom

Kinfolk

Lost Cub

Alpha

Silver Pack

Ronin

Klaive

Impergium

War of Rage

The Umbra

Umbra

Spirits, enigmas

Rite

Realm

Rite of Passage

Rite of Binding

Rite of the Fetish

Fetish

Celestine

Incarna

Spirit (Jaggling, Gaffling)

Totem

Deep Umbra

Dark Umbra

Middle Umbra

Moon Bridge

Umbral Realms

Abyss

Aetherial Realm

Arcadia Gateway

Atrocity Realm

Battleground

CyberRealm

Erebus

Flux

Legendary Realm

Pangaea

The Scar

Summer Country

Wolfhome

Malfeas

Gaia and Nature

Gaia

The glyph for Gaia is perhaps the Garou's most familiar and commonly used glyph. It means not only Gaia the Celestine, but also earth, life, peace, all that is good — one simple claw mark defines everything that the Garou are willing to die, suffer and fight for, no matter the odds.

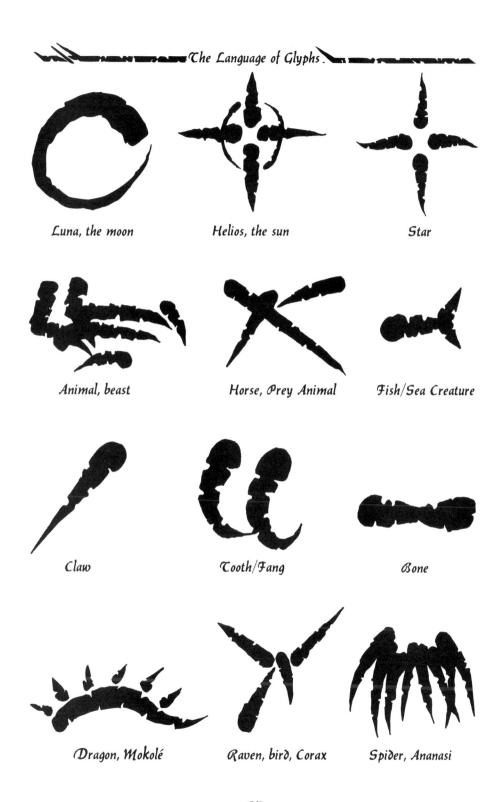

Luna, the moon

Helios, the sun

Star

Animal, beast

Horse, Prey Animal

Fish/Sea Creature

Claw

Tooth/Fang

Bone

Dragon, Mokolé

Raven, bird, Corax

Spider, Ananasi

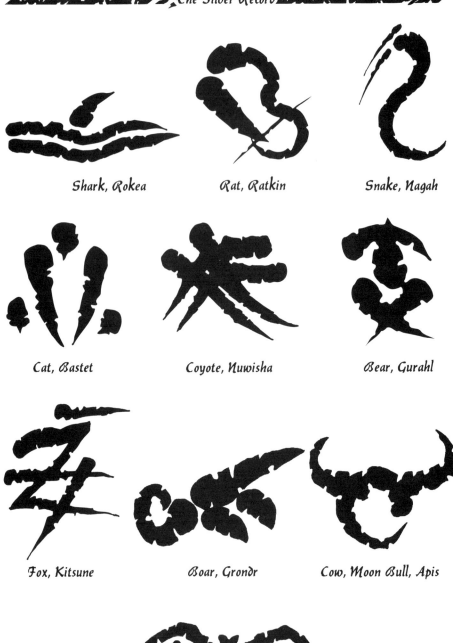

Shark, Rokea

Rat, Ratkin

Snake, Nagah

Cat, Bastet

Coyote, Nuwisha

Bear, Gurahl

Fox, Kitsune

Boar, Grondr

Cow, Moon Bull, Apis

Bat, Camazotz

Wilderness

Forest

Mountain

Desert/Wasteland

Air, wind

Earth

Fire

Water

Metal; silver
(neutral connotations)

Dark

Stone

Tree

99

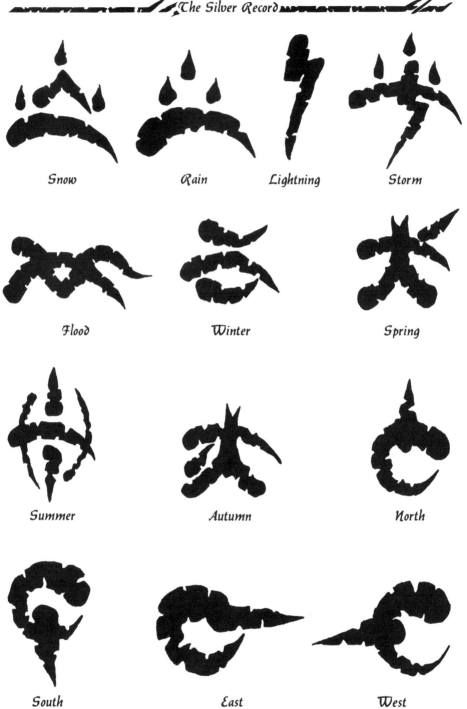

Snow   Rain   Lightning   Storm

Flood   Winter   Spring

Summer   Autumn   North

South   East   West

Totems

Pegasus

Rat

Unicorn

Stag

Fenris

Cockroach

Griffin

Grandfather Thunder

Owl

Falcon

Chimera

Uktena

Wendigo

The Planets/Zodiac Signs

Mercury/Mitanu

Vulcan/Hakahe

Venus/Tambiyah

Mars/Nerigal

Earth/Eshtarra

Asteroid belt/Rorg

Jupiter/Zarok

Saturn/LuBat

Uranus/Ruatma

Neptune/Shantar

Pluto/Meros

Moon/Sokhta

Sun/Katanka-Sonnak

Red Star/Anthelios

Silver Fang Specific

Lodge of the Moon

Lodge of the Sun

House Austere Howl

House Blood-Red Crest

House Crescent Moon

House Gleaming Eye

House Unbreakable Hearth

House Wise Heart

House Wyrmfoe

Siberakh

The Wyrm

Wyrm

The glyph for "Wyrm" connotes pure evil; it is the Garou's best way of expressing enemy, evil, hatred, malice, decay, and most other things of such nature. When a werewolf growls that something "smells of the Wyrm," it is because that's the best way that human language can express what the effect of scenting violation and corruption and rot is like. Outsiders, of course, have a tendency to take this literally, and presume that werewolves blame everything from toxic waste spills to parking tickets on the Wyrm. But then again, to outsiders, "Wyrm" is just a word. To Garou, it is a smell, a feeling, an acidic taste — it is palpable decay, and to them, no word better carries such an impact.

| Defiler Wyrm, pollution, atrocity, violation | Beast-of-War, warfare, slaughter | Eater-of-Souls, gluttony |

Apocalypse

Black Spiral Dancers

Fomor, fomori

Bane

Urge Wyrm

Monsters

Vampire

Abomination

Hive

Radiation

Toxic Waste

Factory/Pollution

The Weaver

Weaver

City

Park

Building

Road

Metal

Gun

The Wyld

The Wyld; also chance, change

Abstractions and Actions

Life	Death	Birth

War	Peace	Sacrifice

Sex, intercourse

Love

Dance

Story

Howl, song

Jump

Hide, conceal

Safety

Danger

Travel

Quest

Create; also used as
artist, author, creator

Repair, mend

Put together, join, build

Suffering, pain

Defiance

Convalescence, regeneration

Therapy

Time, past, present, future

Cycle, recurrence

Modifiers

Ancient, the First Times

Branded, scarred, scar

Coward/weakling

Pregnant

Friend/ally

Rival

Brutally destructive; silver
(connotations of hurtful, and
sometimes purifying)

Sharp, fang

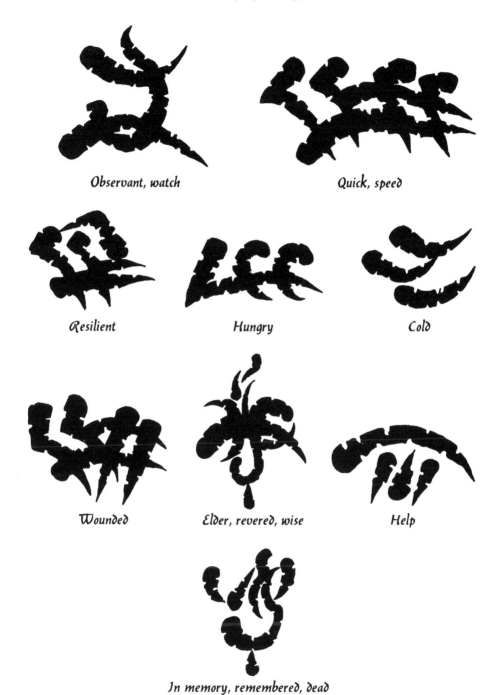

Observant, watch

Quick, speed

Resilient

Hungry

Cold

Wounded

Elder, revered, wise

Help

In memory, remembered, dead

Appendix One: The Other Breeds

As much as the other Changing Breeds might be loath to admit it, the Garou have the most detailed and complete system of shapechanger-specific writing, bar none. Certainly this has something to do with the cultures of the werebeasts involved; not one Changing Breed has the sort of group mentality that the werewolves possess. Whether they envy it or dismiss it, there's no denying that the Garou's pictoral code is the slickest one available.

Some shapeshifters are content to emulate the werewolves' own glyphs. Nuwisha in particular are notable for borrowing the Garou's pictograms in full, although the smaller size of their claws makes it difficult for them to create perfect forgeries. Likewise, the Gurahl claim to have shared the Garou's writing system with them from the beginning of time, although the werebears use it much less frequently. If for no other reason, there's no mistaking a pictogram carved with bearlike claws, and the Gurahl are hesitant to call attention to what limited presence they have left. The Kitsune study Garou pictograms with great fervor, but count the werewolves' marks as only one of several forms of writing that are worthy of attention. These three Breeds are the most likely to be able understand Garou glyphs; any others must try to gather the pictograms' meaning the hard way.

Others argue that they have no need for race-specific pictograms at all. Among these, most certainly, are the Mokolé; the children of Dragon have no need for mnemonics when their ancestral memory will serve. Their distant cousins, the Nagah, rely on a purely oral tradition, memorizing sweeping epics and moralistic fables in the form of exquisite songs. Ratkin live almost completely in the "now," and have few memories they care to cherish; the Ananasi prefer encrypted forms of human writing to a language of their own. And the Rokea are so long-lived that it's not difficult for them to learn what ancestral memories they need — and it's not as if their preferred habitat is rich with permanent writing surfaces, anyway.

That leaves but two: the Bastet, and the Corax. Both have developed their own codes and markings, and although their vocabulary is rather more limited, it certainly gets the needed point across without being too obvious. That's all the Cats and Ravens ask.

Bastet

The Bastet have their own system of glyphs, although it's much less elaborate than the Garou's. In fact, given the extremely solitary nature of most Bastet, almost all the pictogram messages they leave boil down to two statements: "Keep Out," and the reason why the reader should do so. Territory might be marked with the "Keep Out" glyph and a mark denoting the owner's tribe; or the "Danger" pictogram and a sign of the dominant power in the region. If a mark appears indicating a Bastet, Incarna or the like but a pictogram of forbiddance does not, that generally indicates that other Bastet are welcome to investigate, either because the glyph's carver didn't have time to look the area over himself, or because the reader is actually welcome. Bastet who find such an invitation, naturally, can't resist the urge to investigate — but they do so most carefully.

The one constant exception to this general guideline is the mark of "oathbreaker." This pictogram is most commonly carved by an outsider Bastet over any and all markings the criminal may have left behind. The inclusion of this mark of shame indicates that Bastet should not trust whatever message it overlaps; whether the oathbreaker's warning is true or not (and they can be quite true), it should never be taken at face value.

Bastet glyphs are carved by claw, in delicate and winding patterns. Like the Garou glyph system, Bastet pictograms reflect the physiology of the carver's claws as much as they reflect her temperament. Unlike werewolf pictograms, they are designed to be carved with only one claw at a time. The Bastet typically etch these patterns into wood, as if sharpening their claws, but have been known to leave particularly dire warnings in stone or concrete. As thin as the lines are, Bastet glyphs are hard to notice easily; Storytellers may well call for Perception tests of high difficulty for players even to note such markings at all.

Taghairm

Nala

Rajah

Cahlash

Seline

Gaia

Asura

Oathbreaking, oathbreaker

Garou

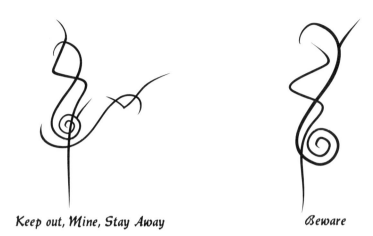

Keep out, Mine, Stay Away   Beware

Tribes

The Bastet's tribal glyphs reflect their territorial nature. Each one consists of a "territory" marking, generally that of a continent, modified by another mark to signify the cat breed at hand. The most common marks are "fury," which indicates the warrior tribes such as Balam and Khan; "knowledge," which denotes a tribe renowned for its stores of lore and secrets, notably Bagheera and Qualmi; and "pride," which marks tribes notable for following their own laws and ways, like the Pumonca and Simba.

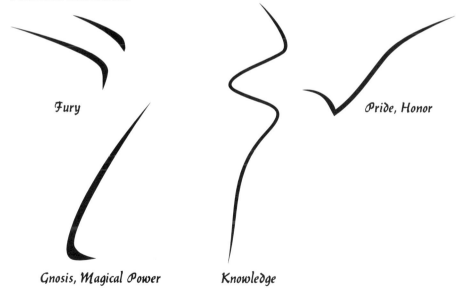

Fury   Pride, Honor

Gnosis, Magical Power   Knowledge

There are exceptions, of course. The Swara are denoted by their territory of Africa, modified by a mark implying their great speed. The Ceilican were described with the glyph for Europe, with the added marks of "wild, fae, Nala, madness" and "Gnosis" to imply their half-crazy, magical nature. The Bubasti, for their part, devised a glyph for Egypt (for surely, they said, it is a territory all its own, not really part of the savannahs to the south) and appended the "Gnosis" mark to represent their magical talent.

Finally, the Ajaba's glyph is not the one the Ajaba use for themselves; indeed, the Ajaba's entirely different claw design makes them ill-suited to carving Bastet symbols. Instead, the Simba were the ones to mandate that the Ajaba be represented by the territorial mark for Africa, crossed with the mark of oathbreaker. To the Ajaba, this is just one more insult added to the litany of injuries they've already suffered.

Bagheera   Khan   Balam

Qualmi   Pumonca   Simba

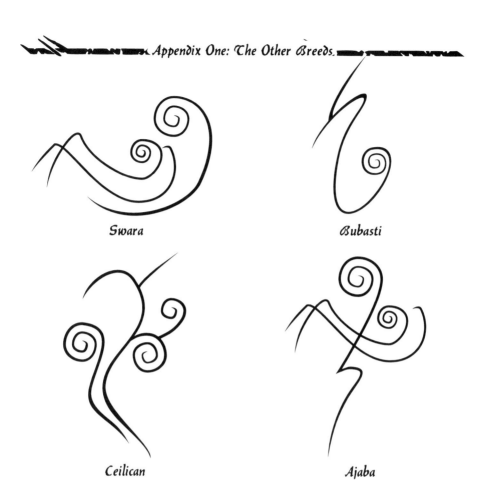

Swara

Bubasti

Ceilican

Ajaba

Territories

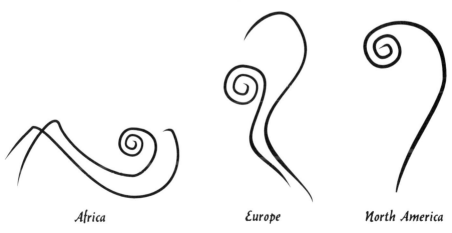

Africa

Europe

North America

South America

Asia

Egypt

Corax

There's only one design principle behind the Corax's system of trail markings: pure and simple utility. The wereravens' glyphs aren't even really pictograms at all; they're just simple symbols, easily gouged out with one avian foot, whose meaning is learned rather than understood. The marks aren't even meant to be permanent in most cases; after all, what's the use of leaving a permanent sign to a gathering that's only going to last for an afternoon?

The Corax are most likely to use their trail markers in the Umbra; the physical world is too cluttered and too populated for them to be really viable. The marks tend to be from six to nine inches in height (carved by a Crinos talon, obviously, and not that of a normal raven), scratched into flat surfaces that can be easily seen from the air. Luckily, poor land-bound creatures are generally unlikely to pick up on those marks.

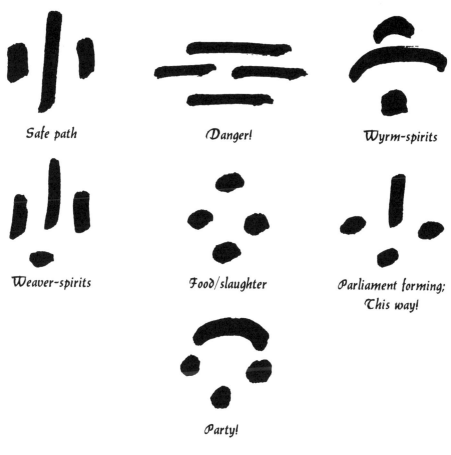

Safe path   Danger!   Wyrm-spirits

Weaver-spirits   Food/slaughter   Parliament forming; This way!

Party!

Appendix Two: Adding to the Record

Immortality

Obviously, the Silver Record is a mutable thing. Even the Werewolf rulebook proclaims that it's possible for a player's character to add a tale to the Record; after all, the recommended Renown award for such a feat is right there.

But how to decide what stories are worthy enough of such an honor? What defines "above and beyond the call of duty" for a warrior race born with the duty of sacrificing themselves for the good of their world and their people? Obviously, the standards must be exceptionally high, or the Silver Record would be twenty, fifty, a hundred, a *thousand* times as large as it is. There's no guarantee that any given generation will produce even one story worthy of the Record. How, then, do you make that call?

First of all, you must resist the temptation to treat the Silver Record as a glorified reward of the Renown system. That's not its purpose at all. The purpose of the Record is to record the stories that must not be forgotten, the tales that teach young cubs how best to carry on with the great struggle. The Renown modifiers a werewolf receives for great accomplishments or terrible treachery are the lion's share of his reward or punishment; it can be seen as a great honor to have one's deeds entered into the Silver Record, but it isn't even a privilege, much less a right. In short, the tales themselves are the focal point of the Record, not the participants.

With this in mind, it becomes easier to eliminate certain sorts of stories. In the twentieth century, it's nigh impossible to enter a new story of battle and vanquishing foes into the Record. Essentially, the response is "been there, done that." By the very lofty standards of the Garou; werewolves are born warriors, and even their weakest can be remarkably ferocious in combat. As such, it's basically impossible to have your deeds included in the Record by virtue of a high body count alone. Killing twenty fomori isn't good enough. Killing a hundred fomori probably isn't good enough. Eliminating an entire Hive single-handedly...maybe.

Also, remember that the Record celebrates the deeds of a pack more frequently than it glorifies the deeds of a single hero. Werewolf cubs are weaned on tales of pack unity and working together to overcome a foe, and loners and Ronin are treated either as tragic figures or as cowards. There's no room for self-aggrandizement in the Silver Record;

Most importantly, a tale from the Record must be somehow instructive. If your pack has accomplished an incredible feat that another pack had done a hundred years ago, and there's really nothing to indicate that your accomplishment teaches a greater lesson than theirs did, then there's no reason to repeat their story with different names. Every single tale in the Record teaches something, whether a moral lesson or a key weakness in a persistent foe. There are a *lot* of lessons in the Silver Record, so there's much less room these days to contribute something new.

The Telling

Certainly, having a tale entered into the Record isn't going to be nearly as difficult as the actual deed that's the story's center. It's much harder to overthrow a Zmei, for instance, than it is to convince elder and spirit alike that the tale of a Zmei's defeat is worthy of being remembered in the Record. Even so, it's not *that* easy to add to the Silver Record; otherwise, the Record would be much bigger than it actually is.

By tradition, the Garou never kept the Silver Record in only one place at one time. Great Galliards, the Keepers of the Record, maintained the history in secret sacred places, rarer than caerns — the Lodges of the Silver Record. There they maintained it in its fullness, passing their duty on from one generation to the next, teaching its lessons to those who came seeking wisdom. Now, in the End Times, there are few of the sacred lodges remaining; depending on the Storyteller's whim, there might be as many as ten in all the world, or as few as one.

To actually add something to the Record has always required a rite, a powerful rite granted only to the most worthy. This rite, the Song of Ages, is one of the badges of office of the Keepers of the Record. It's almost impossible to find a ritemaster who knows this rite at any sept; only a few remain.

For this and other reasons, the rite is traditionally performed only at concolations, where representatives from many tribes can hear the tale and speak for or against its veracity. However, the final decision of whether the tale merits inclusion or not belongs to the Keeper in attendance. Sometimes the Keeper himself hears the tale for the first time at the moot, as another Galliard bears the story to her nation. If he Keeper has heard the story beforehand and deemed it worthy, he may sing the tale to the assembled Garou even as he performs the rite, that they may hear it for the first time as it enters into the Record forever.

The Song of Ages

Level Five

This rite, available only to Keepers of the Silver Record (who themselves must be Galliards of Athro rank or greater) or their students, spiritually empowers a tale, binding it to the greater body of the Silver Record. The ritemaster sings or chants the tale as he claws the story in pictogram form into a sanctified surface, preferably with as many onlookers and listeners as possible. When the tale is ended, the ritemaster bows to the four directions, then leads the assembled Garou in a mighty howl of acknowledgement.

System: The ritemaster rolls Charisma + Rituals, difficulty 7. If successful, the tale itself gains a kind of spirit-essence, and is borne by the spirits to wherever a copy of the Silver Record might reside. The spirits don't tell the story to whatever listeners might be there, unless they are Keepers of the Record; in that case, the spirits draw out the story in glowing pictograms that only the Keeper can see, while whispering the tale in her ear. The pictograms are only temporary, so the listening Keeper carves the glyphs of the tale while repeating the words of the story. If no such qualified listener is present, then the spirits remain dormant until an anointed Keeper arrives to claim the knowledge. It's very likely that forgotten Lodges of the Silver Record still exist in hidden areas, with spirit attendants patiently awaiting the arrival of a new Keeper.

Tales thus inscribed in the Record retain their spirit essence, although not Penumbrally, as long as the stories are told. Rumor has it that the Keepers know the route to a pocket Realm where the Record exists in purest, truest spirit form, and that they voyage there to refresh their memory or simply for pure "reading" pleasure from time to time.

An Ending

Finally, remember that having one's deeds entered into the Silver Record is essentially the ultimate honor that a Garou can earn — that, or the ultimate shame, depending on the nature of the tale. A werewolf can ask for no greater recognition, because no greater recognition exists. The Record is immortality, pure and simple; as long as the Garou survive, so will the names of their heroes and traitors. Be aware, Storytellers, that if your players take part in a tale that is ultimately entered into the Record, there's no guarantee that any subsequent story can equal such a tale, much less top it. Having a pack immortalized in the Record might be the best and most glorious way to end a chronicle before starting anew with a fresh pack in a fresh locale; whether the tale ends in victory or in tragedy, it will be something worth remembering for the rest of the Garou's days.

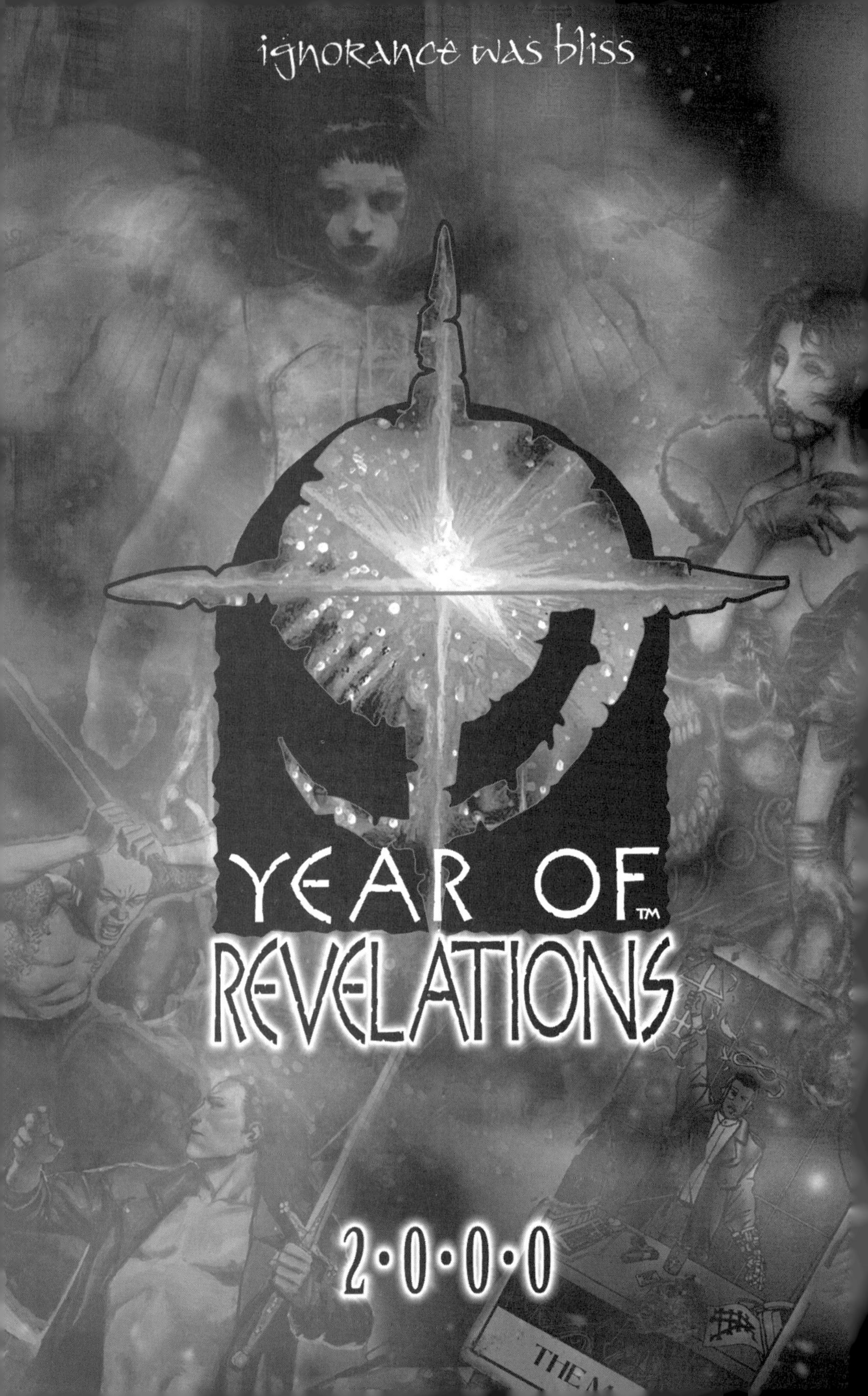
ignorance was bliss
YEAR OF™
REVELATIONS
2·0·0·0

HUNTER
THE RECKONING

WHITE WOLF
GAME STUDIO

Taking back the night,
one monster at a time.

GLENN FABRY
·98·

WORLD OF
DARKNESS

WEREWOLF
THE APOCALYPSE
the HEART of GAIA

COMING
FALL 1999
TO PC CD-ROM

ASC GAMES

Windows® 95 PC CD-ROM

POWERED BY Unreal TECHNOLOGY

RATING PENDING RP CONTENT RATED BY ESRB

WWW.ASCGAMES.COM

Werewolf:The Apocalypse™ is a trademark of White Wolf Publishing, Inc. ©BetaSoft Games Ltd. ASC Games® is a registered trademark of American Softworks Corporation. ©1999, Werewolf: The Apocalypse™ is developed by DreamForge Intertainment, Inc. Windows® 95 is a registered trademark of Microsoft Corporation. The ratings icon is a trademark of the Interactive Digital Software Association. All rights reserved.